THIS BOOK
BELONGS TO:

_____

_____

A VERY LITTLE CHILD'S
BOOK OF STORIES

CHILDREN'S CLASSICS

This unique series of Children's Classics™ features accessible and highly readable texts paired with the work of talented and brilliant illustrators of bygone days to create fine editions for today's parents and children to rediscover and treasure. Besides being a handsome addition to any home library, this series features genuine bonded-leather spines stamped in gold, full-color illustrations, and high-quality acid-free paper that will enable these books to be passed from one generation to the next.

A VERY LITTLE CHILD'S BOOK OF STORIES

WRITTEN AND COMPILED BY
ADA M. SKINNER
AND
ELEANOR L. SKINNER

ILLUSTRATED IN COLOR BY
JESSIE WILLCOX SMITH

CHILDREN'S CLASSICS
New York

This 1990 edition is published by Children's Classics, a division of dilithium Press, Ltd.,
distributed by Outlet Book Company, Inc., a Random House Company,
225 Park Avenue South, New York, New York 10003, by arrangement
with Dodd, Mead & Company, Inc.

DILITHIUM is a registered trademark
and CHILDREN'S CLASSICS is a trademark of dilithium Press, Ltd.

Printed and bound in the United States of America

ISBN 0-517-69332-1

8 7 6 5 4 3 2 1

Cover design by Jean Krulis.

CONTENTS

THE LITTLE CHILD OUT OF DOORS

v

CONTENTS

IN THE NURSERY WITH MOTHER GOOSE

GRANDMOTHER'S FIRESIDE TALES

CONTENTS

ACKNOWLEDGMENTS

Thanks are due to the following authors and publishers for permission to use valuable copyright material in this book:

Robert Gordon Anderson for "The Animals' Birthday Party," from "Half-Past Seven O'Clock Stories," published by G. P. Putnam's Sons; the Milton Bradley Company for "The Pigeon's Visit to the Farm," from "Kindergarten Review"; Louise M. Oglevee for "An Easter Surprise"; Maud M. Grant and The Southern Publishing Company for "Red, White, and Blue," from "The Pleasant Land of Play"; Mrs. M. A. Lane and Ginn and Company for "Tabby and the Mice," from "The Jones Second Reader"; The Congregational Publishing Society for "Ned's Visit to His Grandmother," from "Story-Telling Time"; Longmans, Green and Company for "Chick-A-Biddy," from "Chatty Readings in Elementary Science," Book II; Rand McNally and Company for "Little Duckling Tries His Voice," from "Child Life"; Fleming Revell Company for a Chinese finger play, from "Chinese Mother Goose," translated by Isaac Taylor Headland; Albert Bigelow Paine for "Mother's Birthday Dinner"; Little Brown & Co. and Katherine Pyle for "The Five Little Pigs"; *The Youth's Companion* for "The Go-To-Sleep Story" and to Thomas Y. Crowell Company for "The Little Ant," from "Fairy Legends of the French Provinces."

COLOR ILLUSTRATIONS

PREFACE TO THIS ILLUSTRATED EDITION

As little children listen eagerly to these tales for the beginning storylover, they, and the adults who read aloud to them, will be charmed by the delightful illustrations painted by Jessie Willcox Smith. The artist has surpassed her earlier achievements in the Children's Classics series—*A Child's Book of Stories*, *A Little Child's Book of Stories*, and, most recent, *A Child's Book of Stories from Many Lands*.

Here again are her children, more irresistible than ever, as they rake leaves, take a pet down to the sea, pick tulips in a fragrant garden, battle the wind with a giant umbrella, or create an original valentine. Their attitudes of total involvement and enthusiasm are infectious for readers of any age, and provide the perfect setting for tales of petite adventures and simple pleasures from another time.

1990

CLAIRE BOOSS
Series Editor

FOREWORD

Parents of tiny tots, attention! Do you love to watch your toddler explore the wonders of the physical world? Does the child in you awake on a soft spring morning when the air is alive with the fresh aroma of flowers bursting into bloom? Do you feel a sense of joy in taking your youngster by the hand or in a stroller to the park on a quiet morning when older children are all in school? And, are you able to stifle your inhibitions while reading to your preschool child and quack like a duck, moo like a cow, or gobble like a turkey, or grunt like a pig? Will you tweet like a bird? (For you are actually instructed to do so by the authors of this book while you are reading aloud from it.) But most of all, do you love to read to your child? If you can say "yes" to most of the above, then *A Very Little Child's Book of Stories* is a must for your children's library.

This collection of stories and poems has been gathered, in part, from a variety of children's books and, in part, written by Ada M. and Eleanor L. Skinner themselves. In their search for material for the very little child, the Skinner sisters have selected three categories in which to concentrate their efforts; the world of nature (the out of doors), stories and poems with Mother Goose characters and settings (if not Mother Goose tales themselves), and stories and poems that center about familiar things and relate the kind of simple incidents that occur in the everyday life of the little child.

In the first section, "The Little Child Out of Doors," much is made of the five senses as they allow the youngster to experience the outdoors: in the Skinners' day, country life was more the rule than the exception, and the majority of the stories are farmyard-friendly. Although a story like "The Animals' Birthday Party" dates itself by the main character's unlikely name of Marmaduke, if we are prepared for such quaint touches of a time gone by, we will find much that remains as relevant today as it was when the book was first published in the early part of this century. On birthdays in general, this story claims:

> ...the fifth, I suppose, is the red letter day. A boy certainly begins to appreciate life when he gets to be five years old. Next, probably would come the seventh, for a boy—or a girl—is pretty big by then, and able to do so many things.

In this, and other tales, there is a slightly sexist attitude taken by the authors which was common in that time.

But these matters aside, the stories are chock-full of all the elements that hold the interest of a squirming toddler: repetition (as in "The Old Woman and Her Pig"), explanation ("How They Sleep"), and rhymes of the sort in which very little children delight:

> "Turkey, come to my party,
> If you don't, you're a smarty."

This, too, is from "The Animals' Birthday Party," and will set most youngsters to roll-on-the-floor giggling. There are also talking animals throughout the book, and strong visual cues, as in "The Baby's Walk":

His little white sack was well buttoned in,
And his shady hat was tied under his chin.

One hand was held tight clasped in his nurse's own,
The other held fast a little white stone;
There hung by his side his new tin sword...

There are enough reassuring passages to give a helping hand to the growing-up process, as in "Bobby's Dream," where a little boy has a foreshadowing dream about what life would be like for him if he didn't go to school. And to top all these elements off, there is the surprise ending of "The Doll's Curls," which I won't spoil for you by telling you what happens!

The second part of the book continues with stories involving nature, but adds the charming touch of having Mother Goose rhymes embellished in story form, with more than a few liberties taken. The very titles will entice the child by their familiar ring: "The Clock Struck One," "Tommy Tucker's Pets," "Little Miss Muffet," "The Five Little Pigs," and so on. But don't expect to find these references in their original form, for each piece has at least a dash of difference, if not a whole story, created from a rhymelet. Even "Little Miss Muffet" has been enlarged to create a conversation between

Miss Muffet and Little Jack Horner. And this version of "The Five Little Pigs" adds a girl and a goat and a rather involved little plot. Thus, the little listener becomes closer friends with the Mother Goose characters. Each story is an extended adventure with already-familiar characters, and the child enjoys each one just as, in later years, he or she will enjoy gobbling up stories in series like *Lassie*, *Misty*, *Pollyanna*, *Tarzan*, or the *Oz* stories. The Skinners have opened the doors to literary heroes for our babies.

The third and final section uses its stories and poems to ever-so-subtly emphasize the joys and loyalties in family bonds, where "getting home" is an often-emphasized longing. "The Christmas Cake" is a child's "Gift of the Magi," where each member of a poor family uses his or her own resources to produce the best Christmas ever. Strong family bonds appear repeatedly, as in "The Three Bears," and the importance of young brother-and-sister love appears in "The Go-To-Sleep Story":

"How can I go to bed…till I say good night to Baby Ray?"

But above all, and throughout the book, Grandmother and Grandfather are deeply revered: it is a pleasure to find this sentiment so strongly reinforced here.

And this suggests another question to add to the list at the beginning of this foreword. Would you like to give Grandma a book which she could read to the grandchildren when she is baby-sitting with them, which would also fill her with a sense of importance and love and belonging to the family unit?

It has been more than half a century since this book was first published. That is far too long a hiatus for one which answers so many urgent needs of the toddler, parent, and grandparent: love of nature, gentle instruction in the values of growing up and the avoidance of its potential pitfalls, meeting and enjoying characters one already knows in new situations, cementing the family bonds and revering our elders while emphasizing the sense of peace that moral behavior and adherence to family ties brings. Finally, it offers the pleasure that even tiny tots can gain from the written word—a pleasure which will grow and enrich their lives for their entire lives!

PATRICIA BARRETT PERKINS

Baltimore, Maryland
1990

EDITORIAL NOTE

THE modern reader may be surprised to discover old-fashioned styles of language, punctuation, and spelling, but these have been retained in order to convey the flavor of the original work.

THE LITTLE CHILD
OUT OF DOORS

THE ANIMALS' BIRTHDAY PARTY

Birthdays are always important events, but some are more important than others. The most important of all, of course, is one you can't remember at all—the zero birthday, when you were born.

After that, the fifth, I suppose, is the red letter day. A boy certainly begins to appreciate life when he gets to be five years old. Next, probably, would come the seventh, for a boy—or a girl—is pretty big by then, and able to do so many things. In ancient days, seven was supposed to be a sacred number, and even to-day many people think it lucky. Why, at the baseball games the men in the stands rise up in the seventh inning and stretch, they say, to bring victory to the home team.

The seventeenth birthday is the next great event. By that time a boy is quite grown up and ready for college; and on the eighteenth he can vote. But after that people don't think so much of birthdays until their seventieth or so, when they become very proud of them once more. Perhaps they grow like little children again. Wouldn't it be funny to have, say, eighty candles on one cake? But what cook or baker makes cakes big enough for that?

Marmaduke wasn't looking so far ahead. All he was thinking about was his own birthday, which came that fine day, his seventh; and he was wondering if Mother would put the seven candles on his cake, and if it would turn out chocolate, which he very much hoped.

About three o'clock of this same day, Mother looked out of the window and said, "Good gracious!" which were the very worst words she ever said; and Father looked up from the cider-press which he was mending, and said, "By George!" which were the very worst he ever said; and the Toyman looked up from the sick chicken to which he was giving some medicine, and said, "Gee-whillikens!" And whether or not that was the worst he ever said I do not know. I hope so.

What could they be exclaiming about?—*Marmaduke!* He was all alone as far as human beings went, for the rest were busy at their tasks, as we have just seen.

But he had some fine company, oh, yes, he had. He was giving a birthday party for the animals.

And this is the way he persuaded all his noisy quarrelsome friends of the barnyard to come to his party:

First he went to the barn and filled one pocket—you see, he was a big boy now and had pockets—one, two, three, four, five, six, seven—one over his heart, two close by his belt, one on the inside of his jacket, one on each side of his hips, and two in the back of his corduroy trousers.   Well, he filled pocket number one with golden kernels of corn from the sack; pocket number two with meal from another sack; and he filled pocket number three with lettuce leaves from the garden; and number four with birdseed from a little box.   That makes four pockets.

To fill the others, he had to make three more journeys—three very strange journeys, so strange you could never guess where he was going.   First he went to the wagon-shed, and there, because it was near the three kennels, was kept the box of dog-biscuit.   Six of these biscuits went in the fifth pocket.   Let's see—yes, that leaves two more to be filled.

For the sixth, he went into his own little room and got a bottle with a stopper in it, one which he had begged from the doctor that time he was sick.   Then he went to the springhouse by the well, and filled the little bottle with milk from the big can.

But the seventh pocket had the strangest load of all. He took his shovel and actually dug some worms from the garden,—long, wriggly worms—"night-wakers," the boys call them—and placed them in a can, and presto! that, too, went into his pocket, the seventh. And now all the pockets were filled.

And, mind you, he did all this by himself. And when he came back from all these errands he bulged out in such funny places, the places where he had stuffed his pockets, so that he looked as if he had tremendous warts or knobs all over his body.

"Did you ever!" said Mother, and all three—she, the Toyman, and Father—kept watching, trying hard not to laugh. It paid them to watch him, too, for they were going to see something worth-while, better than a "movie," better even than a circus.

Well, after all the errands were over, Marmaduke collected some shingles, and all the cups and tins in which the Three Happy Children made mud-pies. And he spread them out on the table in the summer-house very carefully.

Can you guess what he did that for? I don't believe you can. I know I couldn't.

Then he took his little scoopnet, and went to the pond and put the net in. Out it came, and in the meshes flopped and tumbled and somersaulted three tiny fish.

These he placed in one of the pans on the table in the summer-house, and then hurried to the rabbit-hutch and opened the sliding door and called,—

> "Come, Bunny, Bunny,
> An' don't be funny!"

But first we must explain that Marmaduke had a queer trick of making rhymes. I guess he caught it from the Toyman, who used to make lots for the children, just to see them laugh. So Marmaduke got the habit. And making rhymes is just as catching as measles and whooping cough, only it doesn't hurt so much.

Of course, some of Marmaduke's rhymes weren't very good, but he tried his best, which is all you can ask of anybody. Anyway, we will have to tell you them just as he made them, so you can see what sort of party he had.

So he said,—

> "Come, Bunny, Bunny,
> An' don't be funny!"

It didn't mean anything much, but he just said it.

And out, hippity hop, hippity hop, came the White Rabbits, making noses at him in the odd way of their kind.

Holding out the lettuce leaves in front of their wriggling noses, he coaxed them over to the summer-house, and when they got there, he placed a leaf in one of the dishes, saving the rest for the feast.

And the Bunnies made funnier noses than ever and nibbled, nibbled away at their plates.

Then he called out loud,—

"Here chick, chick, chick,
Come quick, quick, quick!"

And all the White Wyandottes came running, Mother Wyandotte and all the little ones, and all their relatives, hurrying like fat old women trying to catch the trolley car. Even lordly Father Wyandotte himself stalked along a little faster than usual, and I guess the Big Gold Rooster on the top of the barn tried to fly down too, but he was pinned up there tight on the roof, and so couldn't accept the invitation, much to his grave dissatisfaction.

Marmaduke put only one or two kernels of corn from his first pocket, in the plates for the White Wyandottes, to hold them there until the rest of the guests could come.

He wanted to get them all together and make a speech
to them, the way Deacon Slithers did when they gave a
purse of gold to the minister. He was going to present
himself with something at that speech. He had it all
planned out, you see.

So next he called the Pretty Pink Pigeons from their
house on the top of the barn.

"Coo, coo,

There's some for you."

And the Pretty Pink Pigeons accepted his invitation
very quickly, and he tempted them, too, all the way to
the summer-house, with a little of the birdseed from
the fourth pocket.

And then he called,—

"Goose, Goose, Goose——

At first he couldn't think of anything nice for them,
but just kept calling, "Goose, Goose, Goose," over and
over until he thought up a bright idea—a fine rhyme,—

"You've no excuse."

And then to the Turkey,—

"Turkey, come to my party,

If you don't, you're a smarty."

Sort of silly, wasn't it?—but, no, I guess that was pretty good.

Then he yelled,—

> "Here Pussy Cat, Pussy Cat,
> You'll have a bite of that."

And—

> "Wienie and Brownie and Rover,
> Come'n over, come'n over, come'n over!"

and at last,—

> "Here, little fish,
> Is a nice little dish."

All things considered, he did pretty well, didn't he?

Now he emptied all the different kinds of food, from his seven different pockets, on the little shingles and the little dishes on the table in the summer-house.

There was corn for the White Wyandottes and Mr. Stuckup, the Turkey, and some, too, for the Foolish White Geese; and meal for the Pretty Pink Pigeons; and lettuce leaves for the hippity-hop white Bunnies; and milk from the little bottle for the Pussy; and puppy biscuit for the three Dogs; and worms for the Little Fish, all placed very politely in their little dishes.

It was a grand party. No wonder Mother said, "Good

gracious!" and, "Did you ever!" and no wonder Father whistled, and said, "By George!" and the Toyman slapped his overalls, and said, "Geewhillikens!"—and perhaps a lot of other things besides.

But there was one serious trouble about this party. Marmaduke couldn't keep sufficient order to make that important speech, which was to have been the event of the celebration.

He stood up on the bench in the summer-house, put his hands in his new pockets, made a fine bow, and began:

"Ladees and Gen'lemen an' all others, Mr. Rooster and Mrs. Rooster an' General Turkey"—but he could get no further.

The White Wyandottes were jumping all over the table, and the Pretty Pink Pigeons, who were very tame, were trying to get in his pockets for more of the feast; and Rover and Brownie and Wienerwurst were jumping up and trying to lick his face; and his grand speech turned out something like this:

"Down, Rover! Get away, you crazy Geese! Stop that, Bunny! Stop it, I say—scat!!—scat!!!——"

Well, by this time Wienerwurst was biting the tails of the Pretty Pink Pigeons again; and Brownie was

chasing the rabbits; and the Geese were flapping their
wings and crying, "Hiss, hiss!" and the Pigeons were flying back to their home on the roof; and Rover had his
mouth full of White Geese feathers; and Tabby was
swallowing the little fish—and—and—Marmaduke was
almost crying.

"I'll take it all back," he yelled, "you're no ladies and
gen'lemen—you're—you're just mean an' I won't ever
ask you to my party again."

Of course, by this time, Mother and the Toyman and
Father weren't just standing still and looking and saying things—they were running—and saying things!—
running straight for that party which had turned out such
a grand fight.

They tried to save what they could from the wreck.
They spanked little Wienerwurst until he let go of the
tails of the Pretty Pink Pigeons, and they got the Bunnies
safe back in their hutch, and the White Wyandottes in
their yard, and Mr. Turkey in his.

But they couldn't save the poor little fish. It was
very sad, but it was too late. Tabby wasn't like Jonah's
whale. What she had once swallowed she wasn't apt to
give up.

Marmaduke felt very much hurt and very indignant about the way he had been treated. As father said, "It was a grave slight to his hospitality."

However, he forgot all about it when he saw the new skates which Mother and Father had waiting for him, and the grand Noah's Ark which the Toyman had made with his very own hands. There isn't much use telling the colors in which it was painted, because you know the Toyman was sure to put a lot of colors, and pretty ones, too, on all the things he made for the Three Happy Children.

There is one good thing about all the animals in that Noah's Ark. They are very cunning and look like the real thing, but, as the Toyman said, "You can invite them to your house any time and they won't fight, or bite, or scratch, or quarrel. They are very polite and well-behaved."

Marmaduke had many a celebration for them, and made many a glorious speech to them as well, and they listened to every word.

So the birthday party really lasted long after the seven candles had gone out, and the cake had gone, too, every crumb.

From "Half-Past Seven Stories," by Robert Gordon Anderson.

BOBBY'S DREAM

Bobby was a dear little boy who loved almost everything. He was very fond indeed of dogs, birds, and ponies, and he enjoyed playing with them. One day he said, "I hope I can always stay at home with my pets. I should not like to leave them even to go to school."

The more he thought about it the less he thought he would like to go to school. He decided that each morning he would have a new excuse. Perhaps he wouldn't *feel* able to go. Maybe the day would be too hot or too cold. It might be raining. He loved to be out in the rain but not on a school day.

He well knew that when the time came he *would* go, for he always did what his mother wished him to do. Well, if he really *must* go to school he wouldn't go skipping along. He would go dragging his feet, looking very sad. Perhaps his mother would be sorry and call him back. Dear! Dear! Why did little boys *have* to go to school?

Father said, that in school children were trained to grow into good business people. But Bobby knew very well that even if he never went to school, he could keep a candy shop. That was what he had planned to do. So why should he bother about going to school?

On his birthday Bobby's father gave him a bright shining rake. He loved it and, of course, wanted to use it at once. It was autumn and the ground was covered with leaves.

"Bobby," said Mother, "you may rake the leaves. I'll pay you a quarter an hour."

Bobby's eyes shone. That was good pay for a little boy. So he went to work. He found it great fun. The leaves were such bright colors. He loved to rake them into mounds.

Presently out came Mother to see how he was getting along.

"Oh!" she cried, "how pretty they are! Let's make a house."

"A house? How?" asked Bobby.

"Why," said Mother, "did we never do that? You'll love it. See!"

She took the little rake and in a few moments had

one square room with a fence of leaves. This she divided into four parts.

"There are four rooms," she gayly cried, "parlor, sitting-room, bedroom, and kitchen. Now we will make a bed."

Soon she had a pile of leaves in a corner of one room.

"That's a nice soft bed," she said. "I hear the telephone. Lie down and rest until I come back; then we will play house."

Bobby lay on the bed of gay colors looking up at the sky. How pretty it was, shining so blue through the branches of the trees. He listened to the wind singing a drowsy tune, while the leaves seemed to be clapping their hands. Then—why, what was that?

A sudden swirl of leaves came scurrying toward him and he saw that each curly brown leaf enfolded a Brownie.*

"It's a regiment of Brownies," he thought as the captain marched them straight up in front of him where they stood very still in one long row. Then the captain cried, "Attention!"

For a moment, not a sound was to be heard. Then they all talked at once.

*A good-natured goblin that performs helpful services.

Bobby tried to hear what they said and after a while the captain silenced them and said: "You want to earn some money? Here's a fine chance for one of you. The captain of a big ship wants some one to go on a long trip with him. A ship is great fun, especially when it sails to places where oranges, bananas, nuts, spices, raisins, and all sorts of goodies grow. The one who goes must know geography very well. Who wishes to go?"

For a moment there was no reply. Then came a sad little voice: "I'd love it, only I don't know my geography very well. I didn't like to go to school."

"Well," said the captain. "How's this? A man who sells prize dogs needs some one to write letters for him. The one who does this work may play with the dogs and may have one of the puppies for his own. He may have his choice of them. Who will take this place?"

"Oh! Oh!" cried the whole row. "We'd love it, but we didn't like to go to school and we can't write very well."

"I am sorry," said the captain. "Those puppies are beauties. Well, here's a man who wants some one to work in a toy shop. He has wonderful toys from all over the world. There are talking dolls, toy ships, toy automobiles, toy farms with all kinds of animals, toy trains that run on tracks! A wonderful place is this toy shop. Who wishes this place? The one who takes it must be a very good reader and read to the man when he isn't busy."

"Oh," cried one, "I wish I could, but I can't read very well. I didn't like to go to school."

"That's too bad," said the captain. "Well, here is one more and it is the finest chance of all. A man has a pony farm. He wants a bookkeeper who knows arithmetic *very* well. The one who goes may use any pony he chooses. One special pet is as black as a raven's wing, with white feet and a white star on its forehead. It is named Silver Heels. It prances around in the meadow with hundreds of other ponies. Who would like to go to the pony farm?"

"Silver Heels!" Bobby cried—"I'd like to go! But I don't know arithmetic very well. I can add, but it doesn't always come out right. I didn't like to go to school."

Then Bobby heard shouts of laughter.

He opened his eyes to see his mother seated beside him.

"What did you dream, dear?" she asked. "You spoke right out loud and said you didn't like to go to school."

Bobby sat up and rubbed his eyes.

"Well," he said, "I dreamed I didn't, but I'm sure I shall love to go, Mother."

"Of course you will, Bobby, dear," said his mother.

Then Bobby slowly rose from his bed and finished raking the leaves.

NED'S VISIT TO HIS GRANDMOTHER

"Mother, I'd like to take Grandmother something in my little red cart," said Ned. "What shall I take her?"

"Here are some cookies I have just made for her tea. Take some of them," said his mother.

"That will be the very thing," said the little boy. "And I'll take her an apple, too."

Mother put a piece of white paper around the cookies and tied it with a pink string. And Ned put a piece of white paper around the apple and tied it with pink string. Then he put both into his little red cart and started for Grandmother's house.

He soon came to a barn. Little White Hen was standing at the door. As soon as she saw Ned and his little cart coming down the road she stepped out to meet him. Right up to the little red cart she went and sniff sniff! She smelled the cookies and apple.

"Good morning, Little White Hen," said Ned.

"Cluck, cluck!" said Little White Hen. That was her way of saying, "I want some cookies."

"No, no, Little White Hen," said Ned. "You may not have any of the cookies or the apple. I am taking them to Grandmother. Come with me to her house. Perhaps Grandmother will let you have some of the crumbs."

So Little White Hen followed behind Ned's cart.

They had not gone far before they came to a house by the roadside. Lying on the doorstep was Little Gray Kitten. As Ned and his little red cart drew near she opened her sleepy eyes. When she saw them, she jumped up from the doorstep and ran out to meet them. Soon she smelled the cookies and the apple in the cart. Right up to it she went and began to sniff.

"Good morning, Little Gray Kitten," said Ned.

"Mew, mew, mew," said Little Gray Kitten.

That was her way of saying, "I want some cookies."

"No, no, Little Gray Kitten," said Ned. "You may not have any of the cookies or the apple. I am taking them to Grandmother. Come with us to her house. Perhaps Grandmother will let you have some of the crumbs."

So Little Gray Kitten followed Ned, his little red cart, and Little White Hen.

It wasn't long before they came to a field by the road-side. In the field was a little fat pig. The pig saw Ned and his cart. So he slipped under the fence and ran out to meet them. Right up to the little red cart went Little Pig. When he smelled the cookies and the apple he put his snout right into the little red cart.

"Good morning, Little Pig," said Ned.

Little Pig said, "Wee, wee!" That was his way of saying, "I want some cookies."

"Oh, no, Little Pig," said Ned. "You may not have any of the cookies or the apple. I am taking them to Grandmother. Come with us. Perhaps Grandmother will let you have some of the crumbs."

So Little Pig went with Ned, his little red cart, Little White Hen, and Little Gray Kitten.

Soon Ned saw Grandmother's house. But just then a little brown bird in a tree saw Ned, his little red cart, Little White Hen, Little Gray Kitten, and Little Pig. Down he flew from the tree and peeped right into the little red cart. He soon found out that there was some-thing good to eat in it.

"Good morning, Little Bird," said Ned.

"Peep, peep," said Little Bird. That was his way of saying, "I want some cookies."

"Oh, no, Little Bird," said Ned. "You may not have any of the cookies or the apple. I am taking them to Grandmother. Come with us. Perhaps she will let you have some of the crumbs."

So Little Bird went along with Ned, his little red cart, Little White Hen, Little Gray Kitten, and Little Pig.

Grandmother was looking out of the window. All at once she saw something queer coming down the road.

"What do I see?" she said. She looked and looked. She took off her glasses and rubbed them, put them on, and looked again.

"Oh, it's little Ned. But who are following him?"

She hastened to the door. There she saw coming through the gate, Ned, and behind him came his little red cart, and behind the little red cart came Little White Hen, and behind Little White Hen came Little Gray Kitten, and behind Little Gray Kitten came Little Pig, and behind Little Pig came Little Bird.

"Well, well, well," said Grandmother. She was so surprised that that was all she could say.

Then Ned told Grandmother why Little White Hen and Little Gray Kitten and Little Pig and Little Bird had come along with him. And Grandmother sat right down on the doorstep and ate the cookies and the apple. She left big crumbs, too,—some for Little White Hen, some for Little Gray Kitten, some for Little Pig, and some for Little Bird.

While they were eating the crumbs she and Ned went into the house. She gave him a bowl of cornmeal for Little White Hen, a saucer of milk for Little Gray Kitten, a pan of milk for Little Pig, and a handful of bread crumbs for Little Bird. And what do you think she gave Ned for himself? A saucer of strawberries and cream. So they all had a picnic out in Grandmother's back yard.

When it was time to go home, Ned kissed Grandmother and said, "We must go now. Thank you for the good dinner."

And Grandmother kissed Ned and said, "Good-by, Ned. I've had a happy time, too."

The little boy opened the gate and went out with his little red cart. Behind him came Little White Hen, behind Little White Hen came Little Gray Kitten, behind Little Gray Kitten came Little Pig, and behind Little Pig came Little Bird.

As they were going through the gate Little White Hen said, "Cluck, cluck!" That was her way of saying, "Thank you."

Little Gray Kitten said, "Mew, mew." That was her way of saying, "Thank you."

Little Pig gave two big grunts. That was his way of saying, "Thank you."

And Little Bird said, "Peep, peep." That was his way of saying, "Thank you."

And Grandmother called out, "You are quite welcome, my friends."

THE BABY'S WALK

On a bright and beautiful summer's day,
Mr. Baby thought best to go walking away.
His little white sack was well buttoned in,
And his shady hat was tied under his chin.

One hand was tight clasped in his nurse's own,
The other held fast a little white stone;
There hung by his side his new tin sword;
And thus he began his walk abroad.

He walked and he walked; and by and by
He came to the pen where the piggy-wigs lie;
They nestled about in the straw in front;
And every piggy said, "Grunt, grunt, grunt!"

So he walked and he walked; and what do you think?
He came to the trough where the horse was at drink;
He cried, "Go along! Get up, old Spot!"
And the horse ran away with a trot, trot, trot.

So he walked and he walked; and he came at last
To the yard where the sheep were folded fast;

He cried through the crack of the fence, "Hurrah!"
And all the sheep said, "Baa, baa, baa!"

So he walked and he walked; till he came to the pond
Of which all the ducks and ducklings are fond;
He saw them swim forward and saw them swim
  back;
And all the ducks said was, "Quack, quack, quack!"

And he walked and he walked; and it came to pass
That he reached the field where the cows eat grass;
He said with a bow, "Pray, how do you do?"
And the cows all answered, "Moo, moo, moo!"

So he walked and he walked to the harvest ground;
And there a dozen of turkeys he found;
They were picking the grasshoppers out of the
  stubble;
And all the turkeys said, "Gobble, gobble, gobble!"

So he walked and he walked to a snug little house,
Where Towser was sleeping as still as a mouse;
Then the baby cried out, "Hello, old Tow!"
And the dog waked up with "Bow, wow, wow!"

And he walked and he walked; till he came once
more
To the sunshiny porch and the open door;
And mamma looked out with a smile and said,
"It's time for my baby to go to bed."

PATSY AND JOCK

Patsy had come with Mother and Father to live by the sea for their vacation. Jock had come, too. He was Patsy's airedale pup. Jock had never been to the seaside before; so, of course, Patsy told him a good deal about seaside fun.

"You will love to roll in the sand, Jock," she said to him. "And you shall go with me to gather sea shells."

"Bow-wow—Bow-wow," said Jock wagging his stumpy tail.

"And you shall go in bathing with me, Jock. That is the most fun of all," said Patsy. "We'll go to-morrow morning."

"Bow-wow-wow! Bow-wow!" barked Jock.

The next morning Patsy put on her little red bathing suit and took Jock to the shore. The tide was just beginning to come in, and when Jock saw a little wave come creeping, creeping along the sand he stood quite still and stared at it with wide open eyes.

"How do you like the seashore, Jock?" asked Patsy, laughing and skipping about on the sand.

She didn't notice that Jock was trembling a little. He had never before seen water move toward him like that. And as the water crept nearer and nearer he jumped away from it more and more frightened. But when it rolled back toward the sea he jumped after it barking and barking with all his might.

"What's the matter?" laughed Patsy.

But Jock didn't hear her. His eyes were fixed on the moving waters.

Soon another wave came creeping, crawling, creeping along the sand. It was larger than the first and Jock trembled again as he jumped back and back and back to get out of its way. Then when it rolled away from him he jumped after it again barking angrily. He barked and barked and barked.

And now came a third big wave pounding its way along the sand. It was the largest of the three and poor Jock was so frightened that he put up his head and howled as if he were in pain. Then he turned and ran away. Patsy knew now what was the matter. Jock was afraid of the tide. He thought that the waves were trying to catch him.

"Jock, Jock!" called Patsy.

He stopped and looked at his little mistress, but he did not come to her.

"What is the matter with my poor Jock?" she cried running to him.

She saw that his eyes looked frightened and that he was trembling.

"You are afraid of the tide, Jock," said Patsy stroking his head. "But it won't hurt you one bit. At home you were not afraid of the pond. Don't you remember that my ball bounced into the water one day when we were playing? You ran in after it and brought it out to me, Jock. You are a brave dog. Come! You and I will sit on the sand and watch the tide. Come, Jock!"

He had stopped trembling now and when Patsy walked back toward the sea, he trotted along by her side.

Patsy put her arms about his neck and said again and again, "The tide is playing with you and me, Jock. It won't hurt us one bit. See! I'm not afraid of it," and she ran right up to an in-coming wave.

After a while Jock lost all of his fear. He stopped trembling and looked into Patsy's face. And the next time she walked close to the rolling waves he followed her letting the water splash on his feet.

"Bow-wow-wow! Bow-wow-wow!" he said.

Patsy knew that he was trying to say, "I'm not afraid now, Patsy. We shall have good fun here."

And so they did. For Jock grew to love the sea as much as Patsy did.

LITTLE DUCKLING TRIES HIS VOICE

Once upon a time fat Little Duckling went on a journey into the Wide World. He wandered along the Barnyard Road, and presently he saw Kitty Cat.

"Me-ow!" said Kitty Cat.

"O-o-oh!" cried Little Duckling. "Isn't that a *pretty* sound! I think I'll talk that way!"

But do you suppose Little Duckling could say "Me-ow?"

No, indeed!

He tried, but the best he could do was, "Me-e-ack! Me-e-ack!"

And that wasn't pretty at all!

So Little Duckling waddled on and on. After a while he saw Puppy Dog.

"Bow-wow," said Puppy Dog.

"O-o-oh!" cried Little Duckling. "Isn't that a *lovely* noise! I think I'll talk that way."

But do you suppose Little Duckling could say, "Bow-wow?"

No, indeed!

He tried, but this is the way he sounded: "B-ack! B-ack!" And that wasn't lovely at all!

Then Little Duckling waddled on and on. Soon he saw a Yellow Bird in a tree.

"Tweet-tweet-tweet-tweet tweet!" said Yellow Bird.

"Oh, oh, oh!" sighed Little Duckling. "Isn't that a sweet song! I think I'll sing that way!"

But do you suppose Little Duckling could sing "Tweet-tweet?"

No, indeed!

He tried his very best, but all he could say was:

"Tw-ack! Twack!"

And that wasn't sweet at all!

So Little Duckling waddled on and on. After a while he met Big Cow.

"Moo-o-o!" said Big Cow.

"O-o-oh!" thought Little Duckling. "Isn't that a beautiful roar! I think I'll roar that way!"

But do you suppose Little Duckling could say, "Moo-o-o?"

He tried but all he could manage to say was:

"M-ack! M-ack!"

And that wasn't beautiful at all!

Little Duckling was very sad. He could not say "Me-ow" like Kitty Cat. He could not say "Bow-wow" like Puppy Dog. He could not say "Tweet, tweet" like Yellow Bird. He could not say, "Moo-o-o" like Big Cow.

He waddled slowly on and on. All at once he saw his own Mother Duck coming toward him along the Barnyard Road.

"Quack! quack!" cried Mother Duck.

"O-o-oh!" whispered happy Little Duckling to himself. "That is the prettiest sound in the whole Wide World! I think I'll talk *that* way!"

And he found that he could say, "Quack! Quack!" very nicely.

THE THREE LITTLE PIGS AND THE OGRE *

There were three nice, fat little pigs. The first was small, the second was smaller, and the third was the smallest of all. And these three little pigs thought of going out into the woods to gather acorns, for there were better acorns there than here.

"There's a great ogre who lives over yonder in the woods," said the barnyard cock.

"And he will eat you up, body and bones," said the speckled hen.

"If folks only knew what was good for them, they would stay at home and make the best of what they had there," said the old gray goose who laid eggs under the barn, and who had never gone out into the world or had had a peep of it beyond the garden gate.

But no; the little pigs would go out into the world, whether or no. "For," said they, "if we stay at home because folks shake their heads, we shall never get the best acorns that are to be had." And there was more than one barleycorn of truth in that chaff, I can tell you.

So out into the woods they went.

They hunted for acorns here and they hunted for acorns there, and by and by whom should the smallest of the little pigs meet but the great, wicked ogre himself.

"Aha!" said the great, wicked ogre, "it is a nice, plump little pig that I have been wanting for my supper this many a day past. So you may just come along with me now."

"Oh, Master Ogre!" squeaked the smallest of the little pigs in the smallest of voices; "oh, Master Ogre! don't eat me! There's a bigger pig back of me, and he will be along presently."

So the ogre let the smallest of the little pigs go, for he would rather have a larger pig if he could get it.

By and by came the second little pig. "Aha!" said the great, wicked ogre, "I have been wanting just such a little pig as you for my supper for this many a day past. So you may just come along with me now."

"Oh, Master Ogre," said the middle-sized pig in his middle-sized voice, "don't take me for your supper! There's a bigger pig than I am coming along presently. Just wait for him."

Well, the ogre was satisfied to do that; so he waited,

and by and by, sure enough, came the largest of the little pigs.

"And now," said the great, wicked ogre, "I will wait no longer, for you are just the pig I want for my supper. So you may march along with me."

But the largest of the little pigs had his wits about him, I can tell you. "Oh, very well," said he, "if I am the shoe that fits, there is no use in hunting for another. But, have you a roast apple to put in my mouth when I am cooked? For no one ever heard of a little pig brought to the table without a roast apple in its mouth."

No; the ogre had no roast apple.

Dear, dear! that was a great pity. If he would wait for a little while, the largest of the little pigs would run home and fetch one, and then things would be as they should.

Yes, the ogre was satisfied with that. So off ran the little pig, and the ogre sat down on a stone and waited for him.

Well, he waited and he waited and he waited, but not a tip of a hair of the little pig did he see that day, as you can guess without my telling you.

THE PIGEON'S VISIT TO THE FARM

Once a beautiful white pigeon flew into Farmer Brown's barn and said to White Spot, the cow, "Coo-roo! Coo-roo!" (*Continue the same low soft tone*) "Oh, ho! White Spot. Don't you wish that you had beautiful white wings and could fly, as I

Up on the house top,
Across the broad sky?"

"Moo-moo-oo," said White Spot. (*Keep the moo tone*) "Oh, no! Oh, no! What would Farmer Brown and the children do without my milk to drink? What would Farmer Brown's wife do without any milk for her bread and other good things to eat? Moo-moo! No, no! No wings for me!"

Away flew the pigeon to the sheep. "Coo-roo! Coo-roo! Don't you wish you had beautiful white wings and could fly, as I

Up on the housetop,
Across the broad sky?"

"Baa-a! Baa-a! Oh, no! Oh, no!" (*Throughout, keep as far as possible the tone of each animal or bird.*) "What would Farmer Brown, his wife, and children do without any soft wool to keep them warm in the cold winter time? Baa! Baa! No! No! No wings for me!"

Away flew the pigeon to Swift, the tall horse. "Coo-roo! Coo-roo! Great horse Swift, don't you wish you had beautiful wings and could fly, as I

> Up on the house top,
> Across the broad sky?"

With a stamp of his foot and a toss of his head, Swift said, (*Here give a whinny*) "What would Farmer Brown, his wife, and children do if I did not draw the plow and the sweet smelling hay, or to market and town often trot?" (*Whinnying again*) "No, no! No wings for me!"

Away flew the pigeon. "Coo-roo! Coo-roo! Rooster and Hen, don't you wish you had beautiful white wings and could fly, as I

> Up on the housetop,
> Across the broad sky?"

"Cluck, cluck," said the hen, and "Cock-a-doodle-do," said the Rooster. "No, no! Our own home we love."

"Cluck, cluck," said the hen. "Fine eggs for Farmer Brown's breakfast, I give.

> Would I fly
> Up on the housetop,
> Across the broad sky?
> Cluck, cluck! Not I!"

"Coo-roo! Coo-roo! All content?" asked the pigeon.
"Moo-moo! Yes, yes!" cried White Spot, the cow.
"Baa-baa! Yes, yes!" cried the sheep.
"Neigh, neigh! Yes, yes!" cried Swift, the horse.
"Cluck, cluck! Yes, yes!" cried the hen.
"Cock-a-doodle-do! Yes, yes!" cried the rooster.
"Coo-roo! Coo-roo! I, too," cried the pigeon; and away he flew

> Up on the housetop,
> Across the broad sky,
> Then back to his own little house close by.

BIRD THOUGHTS

I lived first in a little house,
   And lived there very well;
I thought the world was small and round,
   And made of pale blue shell.

I lived next in a little nest,
   Nor needed any other;
I thought the world was made of straw,
   And brooded by my mother.

One day I fluttered from the nest,
   To see what I could find.
I said, "The world is made of leaves,
   I have been very blind."

At length I flew beyond the tree,
   Quite fit for grown-up labors.
I don't know how the world is made,
   And neither do my neighbors.

AN EASTER SURPRISE

Mother watched Paul walk slowly up and down in front of the house. It was very early in the springtime, so early that the birds had not yet come back from the South and the trees had no leaves. But the sun was warm and bright and seemed to be trying to tell the world that winter was over. By and by Paul wanted something to play with, so Mother gave him a flower pot full of sand and an old spoon, and he sat on the sunny porch.

Every year Mother had a large bed of beautiful tulips. Paul did not know about the tulips, for he was only three years old. But he saw the big round place in the front yard where there was no grass, and it looked nice and soft to dig in. So he emptied his pot of sand into his little wagon, and filled it up again with soft dirt from the tulip bed. He did this over and over until the wagon was full.

The long street was very quiet, with nobody in sight. So the little boy with his wagon walked slowly down to the corner. Just around the corner on the other side was a tiny house. It had a wee front yard and right in the middle of it was a flower bed. There was no fence, so Paul walked in, and sitting down on the ground began to dig with a sharp stick that he had found.

In his wagon were some round brown things that had been in the tulip bed. When he had made a little round hole he put one of them into it and covered it up. Then he made more round holes and put in all of the brown balls that were in his wagon. He did not know it, but the brown balls were tulip bulbs. He was still playing happily when his mother missed him and came after him.

That afternoon the little old lady who lived in the little house sat looking sadly out of the window at her flower bed.

"We'll have no flowers this year," she thought, for the little old man who made the flower bed was very, very ill, and the little woman was too busy taking care of him to plant flowers.

There were rainy days, and even a snowy one, and then more warm, sunny days. One happy day the little old man was better and the little old lady sat resting for a minute. She happened to look out at the flower bed, and what should she see but something growing!

"It must be weeds," she said, and she put her shawl over her head and ran out to see.

How her eyes did shine when she found not weeds, but a row of tulips almost ready to bloom.

"Oh, oh, oh!" she cried, "how did they ever get there? What a beautiful surprise they will be for Father!"

On Easter Day the big easy-chair was pushed over by the window, and the little old man was to sit up in it for an hour. The dear little old woman was so excited that she could scarcely wait. When everything was ready she pulled back the curtains and let him look out.

"Why, Mother," he cried, "where did you get them?" For the tulips were in full bloom, and, oh, so beautiful— red tulips all in a row swaying in the warm spring breeze!

"I do not know where they came from," she said, looking at the flowers with eyes full of love. "They are our Easter surprise."

"Somebody must love us even if we are old and poor," said the old man.

"I never was so happy in my life," said the little old woman softly.

THE DOLL'S CURLS

One bright spring morning Peggy took her playthings out under the tree. She had a doll, a little table, two chairs, and a set of dishes. Her mother gave her some milk and some tiny cakes which she had baked for her little girl. There, under the tree, Peggy and her doll with the golden curls had a little tea party.

"Peggy, Peggy," some one called from the house. Looking up she saw Grandmother who had come to pay a visit. Of course Peggy ran to the house to see her, leaving her doll, her little table and chairs, and her set of dishes under the tree.

Grandmother had so many pleasant things to talk about that Peggy forgot her playthings. All night long the doll with the golden curls lay on the grass under the tree.

But in the morning when Peggy wakened she remembered where she had left her playthings. As soon as she was dressed she ran to the tree to see if they were still where she had left them.

There were the table, the two chairs, the dishes; and

there, lying on the grass under the tree, was the doll. But when Peggy picked up her doll she burst into tears, crying, "My doll has lost her golden curls! Who has taken them?"

When Mother heard her little girl crying she called out, "What is the matter, Peggy?"

"My poor doll has no curls," she cried. "She lost them in the night."

"We will try to find them," said Mother.

They looked in the garden; they searched in the grass; they looked everywhere. But they could not find the doll's lost curls.

"We will make a little red hood for her," said Mother. "She will look like Little Red Riding Hood, then."

Mother made a little red hood and put it on the doll. And Peggy was happy once more.

Spring went and summer came, and no one had seen the doll's lost curls.

"Woo-oo-oo!" blew the wind one day when Peggy was in the garden under the big tree where she liked to play. "Woo-oo-oo!" blew the wind, and the branches of the tree swayed this way and that way.

Suddenly something dropped from one of the branches right down at Peggy's feet. It was a bird's nest.

"I'll take it and show it to Mother," thought Peggy. The little girl picked it up and ran into the house.

"It is an old nest," said Mother when she saw it. "The little birds left it long ago. But what is this woven in the side of the nest?" she asked taking hold of some soft hair. Then Mother burst out laughing.

"I know a good story," she said.

"Tell it to me, Mother," laughed Peggy.

"One night last spring," said Mother, "a little girl left her doll lying on the grass. The dew wet the doll's golden curls and loosened them from the doll's head. Early the next morning a little bird flew under the tree where the doll was lying. She was hunting for something soft and warm with which to line her nest. Soon her bright eyes saw the shining curls. She took them in her bill and away she flew with them to the tree tops. See how carefully she wove them into the side of the nest." And Mother showed Peggy the soft lining.

"They're my doll's curls," cried Peggy clapping her hands. "And *I'm* the little girl who left the doll under the tree!"

It was autumn and the ground was covered with leaves.

Page 35

His eyes looked frightened and he was trembling.

Page 51

"Yes," said Mother. "Your curls helped to keep some little birds warm."

"That was a good story, Mother," said the little girl.

LITTLE BIRDIE

What does little birdie say,
In her nest, at peep of day?
  "Let me fly," says little birdie,
  "Mother, let me fly away."—
"Birdie, rest a little longer,
Till the little wings are stronger."
So she rests a little longer,
  Then she flies away.

What does little baby say,
In her bed, at peep of day?
  Baby says, like little birdie,
  "Let me rise and fly away."—
"Baby, sleep a little longer.
Till the little limbs are stronger.
If she sleeps a little longer,
  Baby, too, shall fly away."

Alfred Tennyson

CHICK-A-BIDDY

Chick-a-biddy was only just born. Almost as soon as he was hatched, and had scrambled out of the shell, he began to peck.

He was nearly as clever at catching a fly as his own father, and quite as quick in gobbling up a grub. But he could not say, "Cock-a-doodle-do" like his old father.

Henny-penny was his mother. She was very proud of him. He was proud of himself, too.

His mother thought that such a clever Chick-a-biddy had never cracked an egg-shell before.

Chick-a-biddy ventured to take a walk, while his mother was busy with her other chicks. He made his way into the barn. There he found a basket in which the cat had hidden a tiny kitten.

"Good morning, Kit," said Chick-a-biddy.

The kitten was too young and too weak to raise its head. But in a squeaky little voice it replied: "Good morning. Who are you?"

"Can't you see who I am?" said Chicky, standing up as tall as he could.

"Oh, no. I do not see yet. I am too young."

"Why, are you blind? I wanted you to take a walk with me," said the little chick.

"Kittens do not open their eyes for the first week or nine days. And I am sure I could not walk, my legs are so weak," mewed the little kitty.

"How funny!" said Chick-a-biddy. "A chick with twice as many legs as I have who cannot walk isn't worth playing with."

Just then the old mother cat came into the barn looking very angry, and Chick-a-biddy thought he had better run away. So he went out, and began to be very busy scratching up the ground when a little bronze beetle crept out from the dust.

"Beetle, beetle," called Chick-a-biddy, "if you don't run faster than that with your six legs, I will gobble you up."

"Will you?" laughed the insect. And then Master Beetle lifted a pair of bronze wing covers, opened out his wings, and flew away, leaving Chick-a-biddy staring at the air and looking very silly.

Passing through the gate, Master Chick next caught sight of a little spider, who appeared to be dancing in the air. That seemed very funny, for the spider had no wings. Chicky was just going to peck at the dangling spider when off it ran up a silky thread, like a sailor up a rope.

"How do you do that?" shouted Chick-a-biddy after him.

"With my eight legs," said the spider, safe aloft in its web.

"Eight legs!" said Chicky. "I have only two legs. Who needs eight legs? I won't believe that any one needs such a lot of legs."

"You wait, then, till you see an old centipede, fully grown! You could not count its legs, it has so many," said the spider.

"Two legs are quite enough for anybody," said Chick-a-biddy.

But just then a strange dog came running after him. Chicky ran as fast as his two little legs could carry him, but he could not go fast enough.

Then he tried to use his little fluffy wings to carry him faster, and in the end he had to cry for his mother to save him.　Brave old Henny Penny ruffled her feathers and clucked so loud that the dog turned and scampered away.

All that night little Chick-a-biddy dreamed of nothing but legs; and to this day he is puzzled as to how many legs one should have.

A WEE COUPLE

I know a wee couple
That lived in a tree
And all the bright summer
Their home you could see.
The bright sun came,
And the bright sun went
And there they lived on,
But they never paid rent.

MOTHER'S BIRTHDAY DINNER

When Mother's birthday came there was great excitement. There were presents which had to be hidden away until the morning of the birthday. But the presents were not the important thing this year. Oh, no! This year it was the garden. Mother's birthday was to be a real garden feast.

The days had become warm and bright. Already the children had been to the woods for wild flowers. Everywhere the trees were tinged with green.

Early in the morning Father had brought in some tiny radishes and some lettuce leaves.

"These are for Mother's breakfast," he said. "You and Prue will have to get the birthday dinner from your garden."

And that is just what the children did. First, there was a lovely bunch of sweet peas at Mother's plate. These were from little Prue's garden. There was a bright sunflower for Father and one for Davy. Prue had a little bunch of pansies for herself.

In the middle of the table was a little glass bowl. It was filled with red roses. How pretty they looked! In another dish was lettuce. It looked like a great green bloom. On a little dish at the side were four round red radishes. They were the last of the little crop.

Soon something came in two small covered dishes. It was something that steamed. When the dishes were opened, in one were peas from Davy's garden. In the other were Davy's beans. There were ever so many, and they were all cooked and hot and ready to be eaten.

But that was not all. Still another steaming dish came in. When that was opened, everybody shouted, "Oh, my!" In it was Davy's corn. Think of it! There were three ears. One was for Father, and one was for Mother. One large ear was to be shared by Prue and Davy.

There never was such a birthday dinner as that. All said the flowers were beautiful, the beans and peas fine, and the corn the sweetest and best corn that was ever raised.

JANIE'S PRESENT

Of course you wonder why this little girl in her pretty clothes is out in the rain. I wondered myself and I found out all about it. Now I am going to tell you.

To begin with, her name is Janie and Grandmother gave her an Easter present. You'll never guess what it was, so I will tell you. It was an umbrella! Not just a plain black one such as most people have. Indeed, not! It was a beautiful green one, and large enough to serve as a little green tent which would cover Janie and shelter her from the rain.

Janie was very happy over this gift which came on the very day when she had other surprises. One was a yellow dress which made her look like a ray of sunshine as she danced about in the yard. With this gift came a hair ribbon, blue socks, and brown slippers. When she wore them with her blue coat she really looked like a bit of rainbow.

This is the reason that Janie wished for the yellow dress and a yellow hair ribbon. On the mantel in her nursery was an odd little house and in it lived a boy and a girl. The boy wore a dark suit and always carried an umbrella. The girl wore a bright yellow dress with a blue coat over it, a yellow hair ribbon, blue socks, and brown slippers.

"How pretty her clothes are," thought Janie. And she begged Mother to give her a yellow dress and ribbon, a blue coat, blue socks, and brown slippers. This Mother did and now Janie was very happy.

Of course, she wished to use her umbrella, and for this reason she watched the little boy and girl very carefully. Why? Because they knew *all* about the weather. They stood on a tiny platform in the doorway of the little house. It was just like a merry-go-round to see them sail in and out of the door. Janie named them Dickie Raindrop and Betty Sunshine.

When Dickie came out he seemed to say, "It will rain before night, so don't leave your dolls out to get wet."

When Betty Sunshine appeared, she seemed to say, "I brought the sunshine, so wear your pretty clothes and never fear that they may get wet."

One lovely thing about them was that they *always* told the truth.

Since the green umbrella came from Grandmother, Janie wanted very much to see Dickie come out on the platform. And when she always found Betty smiling at her, she would say: "Your little brother ought to come out sometime. Don't you think he would like a ride, too?"

One day something happened. When the maid was dusting she dropped the little weather house. Dickie Raindrop and Betty Sunshine rolled out and lay on the floor looking up at her.

"Oh, my!" said the maid. "I must mend the little weather house."

She ran for the glue and soon Dickie and Betty were back on the platform, as happy as ever, only they weren't where they belonged!

They had changed places! Betty Sunshine was on the rainy day side. So if she came out, it just had to rain. Dickie Raindrop was on the sunny side. If he came out no matter if he did have an umbrella, the sun had to shine.

That very day Janie went to a party. She wanted to wear her pretty new clothes. Betty Sunshine was out, so, of course, it was to be a nice day. Janie was in a hurry and she never noticed that Betty had changed places with her brother, Dickie Raindrop.

"I'm glad to see you," she said. "I'm going to a party and I won't need my umbrella, but I shall take it to show my playmates because it's *so* pretty."

She waved good-by to Betty and away she went.

She had a very good time at the party and on the way home she planned to tell Mother all about it. As she walked along, she felt a drop of rain, then another, and then another. Oh, what joy! She raised her big green umbrella just in time to keep off a pelting shower. And all the way home she was very happy because she had taken her umbrella. It was great fun to hear the rain dripping on the big green silk covering.

At home she ran in to see Betty Sunshine. She shook her little finger at her saying: "Betty, you didn't tell the truth."

"She couldn't help it," said Mother coming in just then. "Anna dropped the little weather house and broke off Dickie Raindrop and Betty Sunshine. She tried to glue them in their places again but she put Dickie on the sunny side and Betty on the rainy side. But after all, Janie dear, Betty Sunshine did tell the truth to you. She always says, 'You will not get wet to-day.' And you didn't!"

"Only my slippers, Mother," said Janie. "But I want you to put Betty Sunshine and Dickie Raindrop in their right places. I love to be sure that they always tell the truth."

THE STORY OF BLUE WINGS

There was once an old apple orchard. It was full of beautiful things, particularly in the springtime. Then the trees were covered with pink and white blossoms and the soft green grass was sprinkled with dandelions.

But there was something in the orchard more beautiful than blossoms and grass and dandelions. Sometimes there was a flash of blue wings above the trees. Then a bird's song rang out sweet and clear. It came from the owner of those splendid blue wings and you knew that the king of the orchard had returned from his winter's trip. The bluebird had come home.

High up in an old tree there was a little hole and there the bluebird made his nest. From the outside the hole looked dark and hard; but inside it was as soft and cosy as the prettiest nest in the world.

There sat the mother bluebird on five small bluish eggs keeping them warm with her soft little body. The father bird flashed his splendid wings through the orchard bringing food to the little mother bird and singing his happy song.

At last the shells went "crack" and five little baby birds opened their big bills and chirped for food. Then how busy their father and mother were kept!

During the summer the young ones learned to fly. They learned, too, a few notes of the beautiful songs they were to sing. Their mother told them that when the cold weather came they would fly to the warm South. Then in the spring they would come back to the orchard with wings that would flash and with songs that would be like the first happy call of the springtime.

When the first cold weather came four of the young birds flew away with their father and mother. But one was left behind. Poor little bird! He had fallen from a tree and one wing was broken. He could not fly. He lay on the ground, his blue feathers dull and his eyes dim.

There a little girl found him one morning. She lifted him carefully and carried him to the white farmhouse. She laid the poor little creature in a big wooden cage and fed him with bread crumbs soaked in water.

In a little while his eyes grew bright and he tried to fly

a little. When he found that he could not he gave a chirp of pain.

But soon with the little girl's care he grew strong again, and he and his little friend had happy times together even if he couldn't fly. The door of the cage was always open and Blue Wings, that is the name she gave him, would hop down to the table, and around the room, always ending his play by alighting upon the little girl's shoulder. He would eat from her hand. Sometimes he gave little chirps as if to say, "Thank you."

Blue Wings had never sung since the day when he had tried to raise his wings and had dropped them in pain. He often longed to go to the orchard and fly through the trees and sing his song.

As the winter passed and the days grew warm and bright, Blue Wings longed more and more to sing and fly among the trees. One day the window next to his cage was left wide open. Suddenly Blue Wings felt as if he must fly and sing or his heart would break. And then he lifted his wings! He flew right out of the window! Through the orchard he darted above the trees, his blue wings flashing in the sunshine.

As he flew higher and higher he sang a song clearer

and sweeter than he had ever sung before. The little girl heard it as she stood at her door, smiling up into the blue sky.

Blue Wings never came back to the cage, or to the farmhouse kitchen, but he lived in the orchard and had a nest there. And whenever the little girl saw a wonderfully beautiful blue flash through the branches or heard a beautiful bird's song, she knew that Blue Wings was near.

JACK'S ROBIN

One spring morning Jack and his mother stepped softly to a little window in Jack's bedroom. Jack put his finger on his lips and shook his head. Mother nodded. She knew what Jack meant.

They pulled the curtain a little to one side. Close to the window in a fork of the old apple tree was a nest. Four blue eggs were in it.

"I see the robin coming," whispered Mother. "She will cover the eggs with her breast and wings."

Jack and his mother slipped away without making any noise.

"I shall look at my robin's nest every morning, Mother," said Jack.

In a few days he ran downstairs as fast as he could go. "The birdies have come, Mother," he called. "There are four of them and they have funny, big mouths. The mother bird is giving them their breakfast."

"We'll help the robin to feed her hungry little family," said Mother.

They threw plenty of crumbs under the old apple tree. Then they went to Jack's window and watched. Jack had to hold his hand over his mouth to keep from laughing out loud.

"I never knew little robins had such big mouths," he said.

"In a few weeks the mother bird will teach them to fly," said Mother.

One day Jack came running into the house. "Mother!" he cried, "my robin has hurt her wing. She can't fly up to her nest! How will the little birds get something to eat?"

Jack's mother went into the garden with him. There chirping and fluttering about on the grass they saw the robin. She had sprained one wing and could fly only a short distance. In the apple tree nest four hungry little birds called, "Cheep, cheep! Cheep, cheep!"

Once the mother robin flew to the top of a low bush which stood near the apple tree. She had something in her bill. But soon she fluttered down to the grass again.

"She is not very badly hurt," said Mother. "But the nest is too high for her."

"She can fly a bit at a time," said Jack.

Then his face brightened and he said, "I know! I know! We'll put a ladder against the tree for her. There is one in the barn."

"We'll try it," said Mother. "Come, we'll ask the gardener to carry the ladder for us."

Away they went to the barn. Very soon a ladder was placed so that the top of it nearly touched the nest.

"Come to my bedroom and watch," said Jack.

In a little while the mother robin flew to the foot of the ladder. She had something in her bill. The little birds in the nest cried, "Cheep, cheep! Cheep, cheep! Cheep, cheep! Cheep, cheep!"

Mother Robin hopped on the first step. She stopped a moment and then fluttered to the grass again.

"Is she afraid, Mother?" whispered Jack.

"Yes, and her wing hurts her, but she'll reach the nest, I'm sure," answered Mother.

Again the robin flew to the first step of the ladder. She rested a while and then flew to the next step.

"Cheep, cheep! Cheep, cheep!" cried the hungry birds.

Step by step Mother Robin made her way up the ladder to the nest. What a clatter there was! How wide those tiny birds' mouths opened! And into their mouths

Mother Robin dropped the food which she had brought. Then slowly, step by step, down the ladder she flew to get more food for them. It was hard work, you may be sure. But up and down the ladder she went all the afternoon. At night she covered the baby birds with her breast and wings.

For several days Jack's robin made her way up and down the ladder. Each day her wing grew a little stronger.

One day Jack saw her reach the nest in one flight.

"We may take the ladder away, Mother," he cried, "My robin's wing is well!"

HOW THEY SLEEP

Some things go to sleep in such a funny way.
Little birds stand on one leg and tuck their heads away.

Chickens do the same standing on their perch;
Little mice lie soft and still as if they were in church;

Kittens curl up close in such a funny ball,
Horses hang their sleepy heads and stand still in a stall;

Sometimes dogs stretch out, or curl up in a heap;
Cows lie down upon their sides when they would go to
     sleep.

But little babies dear are snugly tucked in beds,
Warm with blankets, all so soft, and pillows for their
     heads.

Bird and beast and babe—I wonder which of all
Dream the dearest dreams that down from dreamland
     fall!

IN THE NURSERY WITH
MOTHER GOOSE

WHAT DAVID FOUND

What do you suppose happened to David before he had his supper? When I tell you, you will know why he seems to be so *very* hungry. The porch where he is sitting is at his grandfather's farm away out in the country. The little girl feeding him is his cousin, Annie. She has no brother and David is like a big doll to her. So she loves him dearly.

Once David found something that Annie had lost. She hunted for it but she could not find it. And now I'll tell you all about it.

When David got off the train with his mother, there was Grandfather waiting for him. Not with an automobile. No, indeed! There he was in a lovely spring wagon and two brown horses with long tails.

David could hardly wait to help drive, for David had never driven horses. So he sat in Grandfather's lap and drove all the way and laughed aloud when the long tails switched around telling the flies to go away. After a long ride, the wagon stopped at the farmhouse.

Grandfather lifted him down and his little fat legs longed to run in every direction at once.

There were so many things to see. First, he had to eat his dinner and then—dear, dear, what do you suppose Mother did? She put him to bed! He wanted to run out and play but she told him to take just a little nap, then he might do anything he liked to do.

He was left alone in the cool room, but how could a little boy go to sleep with so many things calling him? There were birds, chickens, lambs, pigs, and even a singing brook. So by and by he put one foot out of bed, then the other. And when both feet were upon the floor he stood still and listened. All he heard was a big clock saying, "Tick tock, tick tock." Every one else was taking a nap.

He ran downstairs and out in the sunshine and fresh air. There he pranced and he danced like a colt. He raced through an orchard. Under a tree he found a beautiful large red apple. He loved the juice but he didn't care for the skin, and so everywhere he went he dropped a tiny bit of red skin.

He called to the chickens, the pigs, and the ducks. He looked through the bars at the cows. Then he found the brook. Here he sailed bits of wood which he called boats.

Up hill and down he went; and finally, as he circled around toward home, he saw a red building. He peeped in and found it full of sweet-smelling hay. Such a lovely place for a drowsy tired little boy! He crept about and here and there found nests full of eggs. On some of them hens were setting. When he came near some hens bristled their feathers and clucked at him so hard that he thought they wanted him to go away.

So he went on, hunting for a nice place to make a nest for himself. That's what the hay seemed to be there for. Suddenly he heard a queer rustling, and saw the hay moving. He peeped over to see what was there, and dear! dear! He found something he had always longed to have for his very own. Of course, this was the place for him to make a nest; so he curled up in a heap close to the little somethings which he had found.

In the house was great excitement. Mother wakened and went to look at David. And when she pulled the covers down he wasn't there at all. She ran out of doors but no David did she see. She called and called but no little voice did she hear. Just then Annie came.

"David's lost," said Mother.

"My kitten's lost, too," said Annie sadly. "I've looked everywhere. I can't find it."

"Well, dear," said David's mother, "you help me to find a lost little boy and I'll help you to find a lost little kitten."

So they started.

"Good," said Mother suddenly as they went through the orchard. "He found an apple. I see bits of bright red skin wherever he went. We will follow them."

And so they did; and the skins led them here and there and everywhere. They took them to the chicken coop, the pig pen, the bars where he watched the cows, and along the brookside where his boats still rocked lazily on the water. Then back came the bits of red skin.

"He's gone to the barn," said Annie.

"He's here," said Mother. "Here's the core of the apple."

Then she called, but David was too sound asleep to hear. Then Annie heard a sound she loved. "Meow! Meow!"

"My kitten," she cried, much excited.

"And my David," said Mother as she found him fast

asleep. "See, Annie! what your kitten has snuggled down beside her."

"They are mine!" said David in sleepy tones. "I found them—three baby kittens!"

"They are Annie's, dear; maybe she will let you pet them."

"I'll give you one for your very own," said Annie. "Choose!"

David was so delighted he hardly knew which one he wanted. Finally he chose a beautiful gray one with white feet and a white star on its forehead. Then they hurried back to the porch carrying the kittens.

Annie begged to feed David. That is why this little boy is having such fun out on the porch with his bread and milk in the blue bowl.

THE CLOCK STRUCK ONE

Sharp Ears was the tiniest mouse in Mother Mouse's family. One day he heard a little girl singing:

"Hickory, dickory, dock,
The mouse ran up the clock;
The clock struck one,
The mouse ran down.
Hickory, dickory, dock."

"Mother," said Sharp Ears, "I've heard the big hall clock strike one. I should like to creep inside and run up the clock. Then I could see how it strikes one."

Mother Mouse shook her head and said, "A big hall clock is no place for you, little Sharp Ears."

But the next day when this tiniest mouse was scampering across the hall where the big clock stood, he stopped and looked. The door of the clock was not tightly closed. There was just room enough for a little mouse to squeeze through. Very faintly he heard the little girl singing:

Tulips all in a row swaying in the warm spring breeze.

Page 65

She raised her big green umbrella just in time.

Page 81

"Hickory, dickory, dock,
The mouse ran up the clock;
The clock struck one,
The mouse ran down.
Hickory, dickory, dock."

"I'll squeeze inside and run up the clock," thought Sharp Ears. "There I can see it strike as well as hear it."

He squeezed inside the open door. It was rather dark but the tiniest mouse began to creep up one side.

"I'll find a place at the top and wait for it to strike," he said.

Up and up and up he crept to the top. Then he waited.

O N E! struck the big hall clock, with a thundering sound.

It stunned Sharp Ears and made his ears tingle. He trembled from head to foot wondering if it would strike that awful *O N E* again.

"I'll run down the clock," he thought. And away he started. But he was so frightened that he ran too fast. Heels over head he tumbled striking his nose with a bang.

Sharp Ears never knew how he reached home. He cuddled up close to Mother Mouse who quieted him, and bathed his nose.

"Where were you, Sharp Ears, when the clock struck *ONE?*" asked Mother Mouse.

"In the top of the big hall clock, Mother," he answered.

Then once again they heard the little girl singing:

> "Hickory, dickory, dock,
>   The mouse ran up the clock;
>   The clock struck one,
>   The mouse ran down.
>   Hickory, dickory, dock."

Sharp Ears trembled a little. And creeping up close to Mother Mouse he said, "The big hall clock is no place for a little mouse, Mother!"

TOMMY TUCKER'S PETS

You know Mother Goose's little boy named Tommy Tucker who sang for his supper. He was very fond of pets. He had a red hen, a white duck, a brown pig, and a black dog. Every day Tommy gave his pets their supper. He gave his red hen and his white duck some corn. He gave his little brown pig some milk; and he gave his black dog a bone with meat on it.

One afternoon Tommy Tucker played and played. He was very tired when he came into the house for his supper. He was so tired that he forgot to give his red hen and white duck some corn. He was so tired that he forgot to give his brown pig some milk. He was so tired that he forgot to give his black dog a bone with meat on it.

Red Hen, White Duck, Brown Pig, and Black Dog waited and waited and waited for Tommy Tucker to come and give them their supper. But Tommy did not come.

"Cluck, cluck," said Red Hen. "I am hungry.

Little Tommy Tucker
Didn't give me my supper.

I shall go and find him."   And away she went.
On the way she met White Duck.
"Where are you going, Red Hen?" asked White Duck.

"Little Tommy Tucker
Didn't give me my supper,"

answered Red Hen.   "I am going to find him.   Cluck,
cluck!"

"Little Tommy Tucker
Didn't give me *my* supper,"

said White Duck. "I will go with you.   Quack, quack!"
And she followed Red Hen.
Before long they met Brown Pig.
"Where are you going, Red Hen and White Duck?"
asked Brown Pig.
And they answered,

"Little Tommy Tucker
Didn't give us our supper.

We are going to find him."

"Little Tommy Tucker
Didn't give me *my* supper.

I will go with you. Grunt, grunt!" said Brown Pig.
And he followed Red Hen and White Duck.

When they came near the porch of Little Tommy
Tucker's house they met Tommy Tucker's dog.

"Bow-wow!" he said. "Where are you going, Red
Hen, White Duck, and Brown Pig?"

And they answered,

"Little Tommy Tucker
Didn't give us our supper.

We are going to find him."

"He didn't give me *my* supper," said Black Dog. "I
will go with you. Bow-wow-wow."

And he followed Red Hen, White Duck, and Brown
Pig.

When they reached the porch of Tommy Tucker's
house, whom do you think they saw? There was Tommy
Tucker fast asleep. Red Hen called out, "There is
Tommy Tucker. He is fast asleep."

And White Duck said, "He is fast asleep."

And Brown Pig said, "He is fast asleep."

And Black Dog said, "He is fast asleep."

Then they all stood in a row and looked at Tommy. Red Hen was the first one to speak.

"Little Tommy Tucker
Sings for his supper.
I will sing for mine."

And White Duck said, "I will sing for mine."

And Brown Pig said, "I will sing for mine."

And Black Dog said, "I will sing for mine."

Then they all began:

"Cluck, cluck, cluck,
Quack, quack, quack!
Grunt, grunt grunt!
Bow-wow, Bow-wow, Bow-wow!"

Their song wakened Little Tommy Tucker. Up he jumped, for he remembered that he hadn't given them any supper.

"My little pets, you are singing for your supper," said Tommy Tucker. And away he ran to get it for them.

He fed Red Hen and White Duck with plenty of corn. He gave Brown Pig a big pan of milk, and he brought Black Dog a *nice* bone with some meat on it.

After his pets had finished eating Little Tommy Tucker heard, "Cluck, cluck! Quack, quack! Grunt, Grunt! Bow-wow!"

You know what they were trying to say to Tommy Tucker because he had given them their supper.

LITTLE MISS MUFFET

Little Miss Muffet sat down on a tuffet
  All out in the meadows one day,
When little Jack Horner came out of his corner
  To see what Miss Muffet would say.

"Good morning," said she; "Good morning," said he,
  "May I share in your dinner to-day?"
"O yes! Jack," she said, as she nodded her head,
  "But I only have curds and some whey."

"O! that does not matter," said Jack with a clatter,
  "I have here a large Christmas pie";
And he put in his thumb and pulled out a plum,
  And said, "What a good boy am I!"

But just then a spider dropped right down beside her
  With his eyes on the curds and the whey;
But little Jack Horner, just out of his corner,
  Soon frightened that spider away.

Then down they did sit and he gave her a bit
  Of his pie, while she gave him curds
And whey cool to drink; and I'm happy to think
  That they left a few crumbs for the birds.

TINY TIM

Once upon a time there was a little shepherd boy named Timothy who watched a flock of sheep in a pasture every day. He was so small a boy that all the people called him Tiny Tim.

Now there was a fence around the pasture which generally kept the sheep from getting away. So you would not think there was any need of a shepherd to watch the sheep. But some naughty dogs loved to chase the sheep and sometimes to kill them. So Tiny Tim was there to watch out for the dogs.

Now Tiny Tim knew the seven sheep in his flock very well and he had given each of them a name. The leader of the flock was a black sheep that he called Baa Baa; and the next was a pure white sheep that he called Any Wool; and the third was a white sheep with a black face and a heavy fleece: this one he called Three-Bagsful. The fourth was a black-footed sheep which he called My Master, and the fifth was a young sheep which he called My Maid and the sixth was a very small sheep which he called Little Boy and the seventh was a very long sheep which he called The Lane.

Where do you suppose he found these names for his sheep?

Now Baa Baa the Black Sheep, who was the leader of the flock, was full of mischief. He was always trying to jump over the fence. Whenever he got clear over Any Wool, would follow him, saying:

"Where Baa Baa jumps, I jump."

And after Any Wool would come Three-Bagsful saying:

"Where Any Wool jumps, I jump."

And after Three-Bagsful would come My Master saying:

"Where Three-Bagsful jumps, I jump."

And after My Master would come My Maid, saying:

"Where My Master jumps, I jump."

And after My Maid would come Little Boy, saying:

"Where My Maid jumps, I jump."

And after Little Boy would come The Lane, saying:

"Where Little Boy jumps, I jump."

And then Tiny Tim would have to go and take down the bars and drive the sheep into the pasture again.

At last he got tired of doing this; so he told his father what a naughty sheep Baa Baa was, always leading the other sheep into trouble.

"Oh," said his father, "I'll put a yoke on him; then he cannot jump."

So he made a yoke of narrow boards and fastened it around Baa Baa's neck.

Pretty soon Baa Baa saw a fine cabbage patch the other side of the pasture fence and thought he would like to eat some of the cabbages.   So he walked up to the fence and started to jump over.   But every time he tried to jump the yoke on his neck got in the way of his front feet and he could not get over.   At last he gave it up saying:

"Oh well, I guess I'll stay here and eat grass."

And Any Wool waiting behind him said:

"Where Baa Baa stays, I stay."

And Three-Bagsful said:

"Where Any Wool stays, I stay."

And My Master said:

"Where Three-Bagsful stays, I stay."

And My Maid said:

"Where My Master stays, I stay."

And Little Boy said:

"Where My Maid stays, I stay."

And The Lane said:

"Where Little Boy stays, I stay."

And after that Tiny Tim had only to look out for the dogs and had no more trouble with the jumping sheep.

MOTHER GOOSE'S PANCAKE

One day Mother Goose made a pancake. Little Bo Peep, Little Boy Blue, Little Miss Muffet, and Little Jack Horner saw it. They said, "Mother Goose, that is a fine pancake. We'd like to eat it."

The pancake heard what the children said. It thought, "The children shall *not* eat me. I will roll away."

And away it went.

Mother Goose, Bo Peep, Boy Blue, Miss Muffet, and Jack Horner ran after it. Mother Goose called out, "Stop, pancake. My children would like to eat you."

But the pancake did not stop. It rolled away. It rolled and it rolled and it rolled.

On the way it met a dog.

"Good morning, pancake," said the dog very politely.

"Good morning," answered the pancake very politely, too.

"Stop! You are a fine pancake. I'd like to eat you," called out the dog.

The pancake said,

"I did not stop for Mother Goose,

I did not stop for Bo Peep,

Boy Blue, Miss Muffet, or Jack Horner,

I will not stop for you."

And away it rolled. It rolled and rolled and rolled.

It had not gone far before it met a hen.

"Good morning, pancake," said the hen very politely.

"Good morning," answered the pancake very politely, too.

"You are a fine pancake," added the hen. "Stop, I should like to eat you."

The pancake said,

"I did not stop for Mother Goose,

I did not stop for Bo Peep,

Boy Blue, Miss Muffet, and Jack Horner.

I did not stop for the dog.

I will not stop for you."

And it rolled away. It rolled and it rolled and it rolled.

Soon the pancake met a pig.

"Good morning, pancake," said the pig very politely for a pig.

"Good morning, pig," said the pancake very politely, too.

"I see you are going toward the woods," said the pig. "Do not roll so fast, pancake. Then I can go to the woods with you."

"Very well," said the pancake. "Come, go with me, pig."

So the pig and the pancake started off to the woods together. The pancake rolled and rolled and the pig trotted and trotted. They came to a little brook that went babbling by. The pig said, "See, here is a brook. We must swim across it to get to the other side."

"But I cannot swim," said the pancake.

"That's too bad," said the pig. "But never mind. Jump upon my snout. I will take you across on it."

"Good," said the pancake.

It rolled upon the pig's snout. As soon as it was there the pig said, "Oh, you are a fine pancake. OUF! OUF!" And the pig gave a little toss of his snout. The pancake rolled into the pig's mouth and he gobbled it up.

THE CATS' TEA-PARTY

Five little pussy-cats, invited out to tea,
Cried, "Mother, let us go—oh, do! for good we'll surely
be.
We'll wear our bibs and hold our things as you have
shown us how—
Spoons in right paws, cups in left—and make a pretty
bow;
We'll always say, 'Yes, if you please,' and 'Only half of
that.' "
"Then go, my darling children," said the happy mother
cat.
The five little pussy-cats went out that night to tea,
Their heads were smooth and glossy, their tails were
swinging free;
They held their things as they had learned, and tried
to be polite—
With snowy bibs beneath their chins, they were a pretty
sight.
But, alas for manners beautiful, and coats as soft as silk!

The moment that the little kits were asked to take some
      milk,

They dropped their spoons, forgot to bow, and—oh what
      do you think?

They put their noses in the cups and all began to drink!

Yes, every naughty little kit set up a miow for more,

Then knocked the teacups over, and scampered through
      the door.

THE FIVE LITTLE PIGS

Mother Goose had a white gander. One day she asked Ellen to go for a ride with him. Ellen jumped upon his back and away they flew over the fields and trees. As they went along Ellen saw a spot of red among the green trees.

"What is that?" she asked. The gander stopped so that Ellen could look at it.

It was a little red brick house. Around it were other little houses. They all looked as if they were made of wood.

Suddenly Ellen heard a cry.

"Oh, what is that?" she said. "It sounds like a pig. I am afraid some one is hurting it."

"Do you wish to go and see what it is?" asked the gander.

"Oh, yes," said Ellen. So the gander flew down to the ground.

It was a little pig that was making the noise. He was

sitting under an oak tree, with his eyes shut tight. The tears were running down his cheeks.

All at once he stopped squealing. He got up and began to hunt for acorns. He ate them as if they tasted very good.

"What is the matter, you poor little pig?" said Ellen.

The little pig looked up. As soon as he saw Ellen he began squealing again. "Wee, wee, wee! I can't find my way home!"

"Where do you live?" said Ellen. But he was making so much noise that he did not hear her.

"Where do you live?" she said again.

Then she shouted, "Hush!" The little pig stopped crying, with his mouth half open and the tears standing in his eyes.

"Where do you live?" she asked, for the third time.

"I live in the little house near the brick house," answered the little pig.

"Isn't that it?" said Ellen. She pointed to one of the houses she had flown over.

The little pig looked at it. "Why, so it is," he cried. And away he trotted.

The white gander flew along beside him, and Ellen went on talking to the little pig.

"Why didn't you see it before?" she asked.

"I was coming home from market with my brother and I stopped to eat some acorns. My brother would not wait for me. So I got lost."

"But why didn't you look for your house?"

"I couldn't look," said the little pig, "because I was hunting for acorns. Then I began to cry. Then I hunted for some more acorns."

Ellen could not help laughing. "I think I will go home with you. You may get lost again," she said. "How many brothers have you?"

"Four," answered the pig. "One of them is going to have roast beef for dinner."

Suddenly he sat down and began to cry again.

"What is the matter now?" asked Ellen.

"Wee, wee! Perhaps he has eaten it," squealed the little pig.

"You'd better hurry home and see. If you sit here and cry, I know you won't get any."

This made the little pig jump up. He started for home as fast as his short legs could carry him.

When Ellen and the little pig reached the house another pig was standing at the door.

"You naughty little pig," he said. "Why didn't you come home with me?"

The little pig did not answer this question.

"Has Middling finished his roast beef?" he asked.

"There is some fat left."

The little pig hurried in through the door.

"Is this your house?" asked Ellen.

"Yes," grunted the big pig.

Then three other pigs came to the door. They all stared at Ellen.

"It is a pretty little house," said Ellen.

"Would you like to look inside?" asked the largest pig.

"Yes, if you please," said Ellen. So she jumped off the gander's back and looked in at the door.

The little pig was sitting at the table, eating roast beef as fast as he could.

"It is a very pretty house," she said again.

Then she looked at the other houses. "Who lives in all these houses?" she asked.

"In that big brick house lives another pig," answered Middling. "Sometimes he comes to see us, but he does not come very often. He is in a story and we are only in a rhyme."

"What story is he in?" asked Ellen.

"He is in the story of the wolf that huffed and puffed and blew the house in."

"Oh, yes, I know that story," said Ellen. "Who lives in the next house?"

"The seven little goslings live there. A wolf ate them once, but their mother cut him open while he was asleep, and they all jumped out."

"Who lives in the little house with chimneys like pointed ears?"

"An old cat. She is very cross. Once she boxed her kittens' ears, just because they lost their mittens."

"What fun you must have together," Ellen said. The pigs looked at each other and grunted.

"We would have fun," said Ringling, "if it were not for an old goat that lives in a cave at the end of the street."

"He is always playing tricks on us," said Thumbie.

"What does he do?" asked Ellen.

"He painted all our dolls," said Middling.

"Have you any dolls?" cried Ellen, in surprise.

"Oh, yes," said Ringling, "I will show them to you"; and he ran into the house to get them.

When he brought them out, Ellen thought they were the queerest dolls that she had ever seen. They were tiny wooden pigs, but they were all painted the funniest colors! One was bright purple, with a yellow nose. One was green with red legs, another was sky-blue, spotted with pink.

"Did the goat paint them that way?" asked Ellen.

"Yes, he did," said Middling.

"Does he play tricks on your friends?"

"Oh, yes; he plays tricks on every one," said Thumbie. "He tried to play a trick on the three bears one day last week. But Busy Bee went into the Bears' house and stung him."

"I do wish somebody would make him go away."

"I know how you can make him go away," said the white gander.

"How?" asked Ellen.

Then the gander told his plan, while Ellen and the five little pigs listened.

"Good, good!" cried the pigs, when they had heard it, and they jumped up and clapped their feet together.

Ellen thought it was a good plan, too, and she said she would do just as the gander told her. The pigs showed her where the goat lived, and then they ran back home.

Ellen knocked on the goat's door.

"Who is that knocking on my door?" said the goat, in a very gruff voice.

"A friend," said Ellen, and she pushed open the door and walked in.

The goat was sitting on a pile of straw at the farther end of the cave. He looked very big and ugly.

"What are you coming in here for?" he asked.

Ellen was frightened, but she tried to be brave.

"I have come to ask you if you won't please go away and find some other place to live."

"What!" shouted the goat.

"You play so many tricks that all the animals want you to go away. I told the five little pigs that I would come and tell you."

"I won't go," said the goat.

"You must," said Ellen.

"But I won't," shouted the goat.

Then Ellen did what the gander had told her to do. She put her hands up to her mouth and buzzed like a bee.

The goat was terribly frightened.

"Oh, don't sting me," he cried. "Please don't sting me. I'll do whatever you wish."

"Then come with me," said Ellen, "and I will not hurt you."

"What are you going to do with me?" asked the goat, coming up to her.

"I am going to take you home with me, and you shall be my pet goat," said Ellen.

She tied a rope around his neck and led him out of the cave.

The little pigs had told their friends what Ellen was going to do. So they were all watching her. Ellen bowed to the animals as she walked down the street. How glad they were when they saw the goat walking quietly beside her!

When Ellen reached the pigs' house, Middling ran out and put something into her hand.

"It is a present for you," he whispered.

Then he ran back, clapping his heels together, and squealing for joy. Ellen looked into her hand. She had the prettiest of the pigs' dolls. It was the one that was painted sky-blue with pink spots.

A NONSENSE ALPHABET

A was an ant
Who seldom stood still,
And who made a nice house
In the side of a hill.
   a
      Nice little ant!

B was a bat
Who slept all the day,
And fluttered about
When the sun went away.
   b
      Brown little bat!

C was a camel:
You rode on his hump;
And if you fell off,
You came down such a bump!
   c
      What a high camel!

D was a duck
With spots on his back,
Who lived in the water,
And always said, "Quack!"
  d
      Dear little duck!

E was an elephant,
Stately and wise;
He had tusks and a trunk,
And two queer little eyes.
  e
      Oh, what funny small eyes!

F was a fish
Who was caught in a net;
But he got out again,
And is quite alive yet.
  f
      Lively young fish!

G was a goat
Who was spotted with brown;
When he did not lie still
He walked up and down.

g

    Good little goat!

H was a heron
Who stood in a stream;
The length of his neck
And his legs was extreme.

    h

        Long-legged heron!

I was an inkstand
Which stood on a table,
With a nice pen to write with
When we are able.

    i

        Neat little inkstand!

J was a jackdaw*
Who hopped up and down
In the principal street
Of a neighboring town.

    j

        All through the town!

*A crow-like bird.

K was a kingfisher:
Quickly he flew—
So bright and so pretty!—
Green, purple, and blue.

   k

      Kingfisher blue!

L was a lily,
So white and so sweet!
To see it and smell it
Was quite a nice treat.

   l

      Beautiful lily!

M was a mill
Which stood on a hill,
And turned round and round
With a loud hummy sound.

   m

      Useful old mill!

N was a net
Which was thrown in the sea
To catch fish for dinner
For you and for me.

n

    Nice little net!

O was an oyster,
Who lived in his shell;
If you let him alone,
He felt perfectly well.

o

    Open-mouthed oyster!

P was a pig
Who was not very big;
But his tail was too curly,
And that made him surly.

p

    Cross little pig!

Q was a quill
Made into a pen;
But I do not know where,
And I cannot say when.

q

    Nice little quill!

R was a rabbit,
Who had a bad habit
Of eating the flowers
In gardens and bowers.

    r

      Naughty, fat rabbit!

S was a screw
To screw down a box;
And then it was fastened
Without any locks.

    s

      Valuable screw!

T was a thimble,
Of silver so bright!
When placed on the finger,
It fitted so tight!

    t

      Nice little thimble!

U was an upper-coat,*
Woolly and warm,
To wear over all
In the snow or the storm.

*Overcoat.

Having such fun out on the porch with his bread and milk
in the blue bowl.

Page 89

He worked away as hard as he could.

Page 149

u

What a nice upper-coat!

V was a veil
With a border upon it,
And a ribbon to tie it
All 'round a pink bonnet.

v

Pretty green veil!

W was a whale
With a very long tail,
Whose movements were frantic
Across the Atlantic.

w

Monstrous old whale!

X was King Xerxes,
Who wore on his head
A mighty large turban,
Green, yellow, and red.

x

Look at King Xerxes!

Y was a yak,

From the land of Thibet.

Except his white tail,

He was all black as jet.

    y

        Look at the yak!

Z was a zebra,

All striped white and black;

And if he were tame

You might ride on his back.

    z

        Pretty striped zebra!

EDWARD LEAR.

FOUR AND TWENTY BLACKBIRDS

Once there was a king who was very fond of good dinners. One day he sent for his chief cook.

"Make ready for a feast," said the king. "Let there be many dishes. And last of all set before me a new kind of food."

The cook went away in great trouble, for she could think of nothing new.

Now, the cook was a great friend to the birds. Every day she filled her pocket with grains of rye to scatter by the wayside.

A little bird heard what the king had said. He told the other birds. Very soon a blackbird came flying to the kitchen window.

"I am king of the blackbirds!" he said. "The good cook has fed me and my people. Now we will help her."

"What shall I do, O king of the blackbirds?" asked the cook.

"Get a pie platter as large as a tub," said the bird. "And make two crusts for a pie." So the dish was brought and the crusts baked.

"Place branches bearing ripe cherries in the pie," said the bird.   And it was done.

Then the king of the blackbirds called.   Four and twenty blackbirds heard the call.   They flew into the pie and hid among the cherry branches.

The feast was made ready.   Last of all the great pie was set before the king.

"Here is a new dish, indeed," said the king as he opened the pie.

Then the twenty-four blackbirds began to sing.   And their song was all about the good cook and her pocket of rye.

"Send the cook to me," said the king.

The cook came, and, behold, her pocket was full of grains of rye for the birds.

"Change every grain of rye to a silver sixpence," said the king.   "And after this let the birds be fed every day."

Then the blackbirds sang a new song.   All the people learned it and sang it again and again.

And it was sung into a book and it shall be sung to you.

Sing a song of sixpence,
A pocket full of rye;

Four and twenty blackbirds
  Baked in a pie.
When the pie was opened
  The birds began to sing;
Was not this a dainty dish
  To set before a king?

NURSERY JINGLE

Oh! the dust on the feather,
And the feather on the bird,
And the bird on the eggs,
And the eggs in the nest,
And the nest on the twig,
And the twig on the branch,
And the branch on the tree,
And the tree in the woods,
And the woods in the ground,
And the green grass grew
All round, round, round,
And the green grass grew all round.

LITTLE PLAYS FOR FINGERS AND TOES

Finger Plays:

> This little pig went to market;
> This little pig stayed at home;
> This little pig had roast beef;
> This little pig had none;
> This little pig said, "Wee, wee!
> I can't find my way home."
>
> MOTHER GOOSE.

> "Let's go to bed," said Thumb-a-Lot;
> "First something to eat," said Point-a-Spot;
> "Where can we get it?" said Bigger-Not;
> "Out of the pantry," said Ring-a-Ling;
> "Let's go and ask Mother," said Little-Thing.
>
> DUTCH MOTHER GOOSE.

> This little cow eats grass,
> This little cow eats hay,
> This little cow drinks water,
> This little cow runs away,

This little cow does nothing
But just lie down all day.

CHINESE MOTHER GOOSE.

Knee and Toe Plays:

Oh, how do you do?
And how do you?
And how do you do again?
And how do you do,
And how do you do,
Say all these children ten.

Only two cherry lips,
Only one chubby nose,
Only two little hands,
Ten little toes.

MATHIAS BARR

Oh, what a silken stocking,
And what a satin shoe!
I wish I were a little toe
To live in there, I do!

KATE GREENAWAY

This is the way the ladies ride—
Saddle-a-side, saddle-a-side!

This is the way the gentlemen ride—
Sitting astride, sitting astride!

This is the way the grandmothers ride—
Bundled and tied, bundled and tied!

This is the way the babykins ride—
Snuggled inside, snuggled inside!

This is the way, when they are late,
They all fly over the five-barred gate!

WILLIAM CANTON

WHO'S AFRAID IN THE DARK!

One night the wind went about wailing,

"Who's afraid in the dark!
Who's afraid in the dark!
Who's afraid!
Who-oo-oo-oo!"

"Not I," said the owl. Then he fluffed his great feathers. "I fly about in the dark to find food. Not I! Twhoo-oo—!"

"Afraid in the dark?" asked the dog. "I watch the house when all are asleep. Have you never heard me bark when it is dark? Bow-wow-wow!"

But the wind kept on wailing,

"Who's afraid in the dark!
Who's afraid in the dark!
Who's afraid!
Who-oo-oo!"

"Meow, meow," said the cat. "I can see in the dark and am never afraid. Meow, meow!"

"That's my time to play," squeaked the mouse. "I go creeping in and out the room when it's dark. Squeak! squeak!"

But the wind kept on wailing,

"Who's afraid in the dark!
Who's afraid in the dark!
Who's afraid!
Who-oo!"

A little boy had gone to bed. When he heard what the wind said he put his head under the bed clothes. As soon as the wind saw this, it laughed, and said in a loud voice to the little boy,

"Ha! ha! ha! I know who!
You-oo-oo-oo!
You-oo-oo!
You-oo!"

THE LITTLE DREAMER

A little boy was dreaming,
  Upon his nurse's lap,
That the pins fell out of all the stars,
  And the stars fell into his cap.

So, when his dream was over,
  What should that little boy do?
Why, he went and looked inside his cap,
  And found it wasn't true.

GRANDMOTHER'S
FIRESIDE TALES

GRANDMOTHER'S PATH

Grandmother's house stood next door to Bobby's. Across the lawn which stretched between the two houses there was a little path of red bricks. It led from the side door of Grandmother's house to the side door of Bobby's house. Bobby called it Grandmother's path, because she crossed it when she came to see Bobby and his little sister, Baby Jane. Every morning Bobby stood at the side window and watched for their daily visitor. And when she opened her door he would call out, "Grandmother's coming, Mother! She'll tell us another story."

And Baby Jane in the nursery would laugh and coo as if she wanted to say, "Grandmother's coming, Mother."

One winter day a deep snow lay all over the ground. Early in the morning you couldn't see Grandmother's path at all; but before Father left for the office he took his big snow shovel and cleared all the snow away from the bricks.

Later in the morning Bobby stood at the window waiting for Grandmother.

"Mother," he said, "it's been snowing again. Look at Grandmother's path."

Mother stepped to the window and said, "So it has. And Grandmother's path is covered again. I hope some boy who can use a snow shovel will come this way."

"I can use one, Mother," said Bobby. "I watched Father use his. Let me clear Grandmother's path!"

"You shall begin it, dear," laughed Mother. "But the shovel is a pretty big shovel for such a little man to use. We'll see how much of the path you can clear."

Then Mother helped Bobby to put on his blue woolen suit, his blue woolen leggings, and his pointed woolen cap with the tassel. She put Father's big snow shovel into his hands and he began to push it through the snow along Grandmother's path.

It was hard work, and after Bobby had cleared a little way he stopped to rest looking toward Grandmother's door. He wondered if he could ever reach it.

Just then the baker's boy came with bread and rolls. He looked a little surprised when he saw Bobby and the big snow shovel. But he nodded cheerfully and said,

"Snow shovel and you, my little man,
Are working hard to-day.

Little by little, step by step,
   You'll clear the snow away."

"It's Father's snow shovel," said Bobby. "I'm making a path for Grandmother."

Then he worked away as hard as he could. And when half of the path was cleared he stopped again to rest looking toward Grandmother's door.

And while he was resting, the milkman came. He, too, looked surprised when he saw Bobby and the big snow shovel. But he nodded cheerfully and said,

"Snow shovel and you, my little man,
   Are working hard to-day.
Little by little, step by step,
   You'll clear the snow away."

And Bobby said, "It's Father's snow shovel. I'm making a path for Grandmother."

He worked away again until he had nearly reached Grandmother's door. He stopped to rest once more feeling sure now that he could finish the path.

In a few moments the grocer's boy came hurrying along with a basket full of groceries which he was taking to Grandmother's house.

He called out, "Hurrah for Bobby and his big snow shovel!"

"It's Father's snow shovel," answered Bobby. "I cleared a path for Grandmother."

And the grocer's boy laughed and said cheerfully,

> "Snow shovel and you, my little man,
>   Had a hard task to-day.
> But little by little, step by step,
>   You've cleared the snow away."

For Bobby was now at Grandmother's door. Out she stepped saying, "What a nice clean path my little man has made for me to-day." She took Bobby's hand and they both walked across the clean path to see Baby Jane.

THE CHRISTMAS CAKE

All the family wanted a cake for Christmas, round and plummy, thick and white, to eat together on Christmas night. There had always been a Christmas cake for the family. When the games were over and the candles on the tree burned low, and the fire in the fireplace danced and sparkled, the Christmas cake was set in the middle of the table. Then Father cut it, and Mother put the pieces on the best china plates. Sister passed the plates, and Brother was polite and did not eat his piece until every one was served. And Grandmother opened the door to see if there were any one outside in the snow who would like to come in and share the Christmas cake with the family.

But this year the family was not having any cake at all. They were eating only very plain bread and butter and good vegetables that had grown in their garden, and once in a while the butcher's boy brought them something nice for dinner in his basket.

"No Christmas cake for us to eat!" said Brother.

"No Christmas cake with frosting!" said Sister.

"No Christmas cake for me to stir!" said Mother.

"No Christmas cake to share!" said Grandmother, and that was the worst of all.

"No Christmas cake unless each one of the whole family can help to give it to the others," said Father, and that was what started the surprise.

Brother had ten cents to spend; and the week before Christmas he went down to the store to buy himself some candy. The barley sugar Christmas toys had come. There were reindeer and bells and bears and little trees as clear as crystal, red and yellow. But as Brother was about to choose ten Christmas barley sugar toys, he saw the storekeeper weighing his sugar in the big brass scales. Then Brother put his ten cents down on the counter and said,

> "Storekeeper, storekeeper, here is my dime
>   To pay for some sugar this Christmas time.
>   Round and plummy, and thick and white,
>   We want a cake for our Christmas night."

So the storekeeper filled a bag with sugar, and Brother ran home with it. There was enough to make the Christmas cake sweeter than it had been any Christmas before.

Sister wanted to play every day of the week before Christmas. It was a holiday week and she planned to make the dolls some new dresses, and get the playroom ready for the Christmas toys. But she remembered the hungry creatures out in the barn that needed food. So Sister left her play and went out through the snow to give the little brown hen some corn and to pull down hay for the cow.

Then she thought about the Christmas cake, and she said,

> "Little brown hen, and mooly cow,
> What will you do to help us now?
> Round and plummy, and thick and white,
> We want a cake for our Christmas night."

And the grateful hen and cow gave eggs and milk. They gave enough to make the Christmas cake richer than it had been any Christmas before.

Every afternoon Grandmother had a cup of hot tea. Sister took it up to her room on a tray. But the week before Christmas, Grandmother decided not have her cup of tea for several days.

"I shall buy some raisins, instead of tea.
Fuller than ever the cake shall be;
Round and plummy, and thick and white,
The cake that we eat on Christmas night,"

Said Grandmother.

Then Mother mixed together the sugar, the eggs, and the milk with the butter and flour that she had saved in the pantry. She dropped in the fat raisins and beat the cake as hard and as fast as she could. Mother was very busy every day, and all that she could give was her work and the careful baking of the cake. But she sang as she poured it into the tin, and when she took it out of the oven,

"Mixing, stirring, and baking so
With all my might is a help, I know.
Round and plummy, and thick and white,
Here is the cake for our Christmas night."

Then Father came home, and there was the surprise,—a Christmas cake sweeter, and richer, and plummier, and whiter than any Christmas cake before. He could save all the money that he had been earning to buy it.

Christmas night came, and the games were over. The

candles on the tree burned low, and the fire in the fire-place danced and sparkled. The Christmas cake was set in the middle of the table, and Father was able to cut it into so many pieces that there was enough for the neighbors as well as the family. And they ate the Christmas cake that was more precious than any Christmas before because all the family had helped to get it.

RED, WHITE, AND BLUE

Jack was a happy boy in winter. He liked to play out in the snow. He was not cold. He had a warm over-coat. It was a blue coat. He had a warm cap, too. His cap was red. And he had some white mittens to keep his hands warm.

"O, Mother," cried Jack one day, "Tom says I am like the flag."

"Why, so you are," said Mother, "red cap, white mittens, and blue coat. Indeed, you are a very nice little flag."

"But where are my stars, Mother?" asked Jack. "You know our flag has stars in it."

"I think they are in your bright eyes," said Mother.

THE TALKING DOLLS

This is a story of two Christmases, with a year of time and a wide ocean of water between them. Which of the two was the better you must decide for yourself.

On the evening before the first one, two little girls sat by the fire that went crackling and roaring up the wide throat of the chimney, and talked again about the good-natured giant that had come to them so many times on Christmas, and gone away again without their having seen him—the giant in the fur-trimmed red coat, and with the rosy face and the bushy white whiskers; the giant who drove the sleigh loaded with lovely things and drawn by reindeer covered with tinkling bells. Would he come again this year, and if he did, could he get down the chimney with that big fire burning?

Their mother thought that he could. Perhaps he would not mind the fire. Perhaps, after his long, cold ride, it might feel good to him. He had so many places to go to that sometimes he did not come until nearly morning. And so, at last, the two stockings were hung on the chimney front, where Santa Claus could not help seeing them if he came, and the two little girls went to bed, not to sleep, but to listen and to talk.

Once they thought they heard the crack of a whip and the faint tinkle of bells, and they called to their mother; but she told them that it was only the ice on the pond, cracking in the cold, and icicles falling from the eaves. And so, at last, in happy anticipation, they fell asleep.

It was daylight when they awoke. They hopped to the floor and ran, barefooted, to the living-room. There, on the chimney front, hung the two stockings, no longer lean, as they had been the night before, but filled with many beautiful things; and between them, on a red ribbon, hung a box that was marked in big, plain letters, "To Grace and Ethel, with love, from Santa Claus."

Between them they got it open, and found inside two lovely dolls, both smiling sweetly. One had hair as black as coal, the other golden ringlets that clustered round her head. Their eyes were closed, but they opened them wide as soon as the two girls took them from the box. And in the hand of one doll was a little note that said:

"Perhaps some time, if you learn how to make us talk, we will tell you our names and the story of our lives."

Of course the first thing the little girls did was to try to find out how to make the dolls talk. They pinched their heads and squeezed their stomachs, and moved their arms up and down, but never a word could they get; and so after a time they forgot about the note, and Ethel named her doll Rosamond and Grace named hers Violet, and they played with them day after day, and loved them very much.

But one morning, when Christmas had long been gone and the summer had passed, and the leaves on the trees were turning red again, it happened that the doll Rosamond fell off the steps, and hit her head so hard that it came partly away from her body. Of course Ethel felt very badly about it, so she took Rosamond to her mother. She looked at the crack in Rosamond's neck, and saw something white inside. Then she drew out a piece of paper that had some strange writing on it.

"Oh, what does it say?" cried both of the girls at once; but their mother could not read the queer-looking words, and so they had to wait till their father came home. He looked at the paper a moment, and said, "Why, this is from a country across the sea." Then he read, "I am Hilda. I am seven years old, and in Heidelberg live. All the year I the dolls make, because my father is dead; but no dolls can I have myself, for all must go to Kriss Kringle, that little girls in America may dolls have. But I have a bird that sings very much. The man gave him to me because the wing was sick, and I made it to get well. And sometimes Kriss Kringle is most good. Once to me he a candy present gave. The name of the dark doll is Grisel, and of the light doll, Marta. I much love wish you, and that the good Kriss Kringle shall many things bring. Hilda Stendthal."

The little girls listened with wide eyes, and when their father had finished, they danced with delight. "Oh, now," they said, "we know what the note meant when it said that perhaps some time Rosamond and Violet would tell us their names. But isn't it funny that their names should be Grisel and Marta?"

They could think of nothing else, and talked of nothing else, until one day their mother said, "It is in Heidelberg that your Aunt is living. Don't you think you would like to send a Christmas present to the little girl, Hilda, who made the dolls? Perhaps if you sent it to your aunt, she could tell Kriss Kringle to give it to Hilda."

They thought it was a lovely plan. It took them a

long time to make up their minds what to send, but at last they chose a little silver watch, and with all their saved-up dimes and nickels, they bought it. Between them they wrote the letter that told all about Grisel and Marta, and what good children they were. They said that because Kriss Kringle, whom they called Santa Claus, had been so kind as to bring them Grisel and Marta, they had asked him to remember Hilda, and take a gift with him across the ocean, and they hoped he would not forget.

And so, on the night before the second Christmas, two little girls sat once more before the open fire and talked of Santa Claus. And to a little cottage in Heidelberg the great Kriss Kringle came, and left such a gift as no other little girl in Heidelberg had ever had.

For this is the beauty of Christmas: that wherever the day is known, there, too, is known the great kindly figure that goes about giving gifts and doing good. Sometimes he is Kriss Kringle, and sometimes St. Nicholas or Santa Claus, but whatever his name may be, he makes people happy, because he gives them the feeling that they would like to make some one else happy.

THE LITTLE ANT

There was once a little ant
    that was going to Jerusalem.
She met the snow.
The snow cracked the paw
    of the little ant
    that was going to Jerusalem.

"O snow, how strong you are
    to crack the paw of the little ant
    that is going to Jerusalem!"
And the snow spoke and said,
    "The sun that melts me
    is a great deal stronger than I am."

"O sun, how strong you are,
    to melt the snow,
    that cracks the paw
    of the little ant
    that is going to Jerusalem!"
And the sun spoke and said,

"The cloud that hides me
is a great deal stronger than I am."

"O cloud, how strong you are,
to hide the sun,
that melts the snow,
that cracks the paw
of the little ant
that is going to Jerusalem!"
And the cloud replied,
"The wind that drives me away
is a great deal stronger than I am."

"O wind, how strong you are,
to drive away the cloud,
that hides the sun,
that melts the snow,
that cracks the paw
of the little ant
that is going to Jerusalem!"
And the wind replied,
"The mountain that stops me
is a great deal stronger than I am."

"O mountain, how strong you are
  to stop the wind,
  that drives away the cloud,
  that hides the sun,
  that melts the snow,
  that cracks the paw
  of the little ant
  that is going to Jerusalem!"
And the mountain replied,
  "The mouse that bores through me
  is a great deal stronger than I am."

"O mouse, how strong you are,
  to bore through the mountain,
  that stops the wind,
  that drives away the cloud,
  that hides the sun,
  that melts the snow,
  that cracks the paw
  of the little ant
  that is going to Jerusalem!"
And the mouse said,
  "The cat that eats me
  is a great deal stronger than I am."

They were all sorts of sizes and colors
—blue, pink, red, and gold.

Page 212

'Tis time to shut our weary eyes,
And say our evening prayer.

Page 227

"O cat, how strong you are,

    to eat the mouse,

    that bores through the mountain,

    that stops the wind,

    that drives away the cloud,

    that hides the sun,

    that melts the snow,

    that cracks the paw

    of the little ant

    that is going to Jerusalem!"

And the cat said,

    "The dog that chases me

    is a great deal stronger than I am."

"O dog, how strong you are,

    to chase the cat,

    that eats the mouse,

    that bores through the mountain,

    that stops the wind,

    that drives away the cloud,

    that hides the sun,

    that melts the snow,

    that cracks the paw

of the little ant

that is going to Jerusalem!"

And the dog said,

"The stick that beats me

is a great deal stronger than I am."

"O stick, how strong you are,

to beat the dog,

that chases the cat,

that eats the mouse,

that bores through the mountain,

that stops the wind,

that drives away the cloud,

that hides the sun,

that melts the snow,

that cracks the paw

of the little ant

that is going to Jerusalem!"

And the stick said,

"The fire that burns me

Is a great deal stronger than I am."

"O fire, how strong you are,

to burn the stick,

that beats the dog,

that chases the cat,

that eats the mouse,

that bores through the mountain,

that stops the wind,

that drives away the cloud,

that hides the sun,

that melts the snow,

that cracks the paw

of the little ant

that is going to Jerusalem!"

And the fire said,

"The water that puts me out

is a great deal stronger than I am."

"O water, how strong you **are**,

to put out the fire,

that burns the stick,

that beats the dog,

that chases the cat,

that eats the mouse,

that bores through the mountain,

that stops the wind,

that drives away the cloud,

that hides the sun,

that melts the snow,

that cracks the paw

of the little ant

that is going to Jerusalem!"

And the water said,

"The cow that drinks me

is a great deal stronger than I am."

"O cow, how strong you are,

to drink the water,

that puts out the fire,

that burns the stick,

that beats the dog,

that chases the cat,

that eats the mouse,

that bores through the mountain,

that stops the wind,

that drives away the cloud,

that hides the sun,

that melts the snow,

that cracks the paw

of the little ant
that is going to Jerusalem!"
And the cow said,
"The man who kills me
is a great deal stronger than I am."

"O man, how strong you are,
to kill the cow,
that drinks the water,
that puts out the fire,
that burns the stick,
that beats the dog,
that chases the cat,
that eats the mouse,
that bores through the mountain,
that stops the wind,
that drives away the cloud,
that hides the sun,
that melts the snow,
that cracks the paw
of the little ant
that is going to Jerusalem!"

THE THREE BEARS

Once upon a time there were three bears. They lived in a house of their own in a wood. Father Bear was a great big bear; Mother Bear was a middle-sized bear; and Baby Bear was a little wee bear.

Each bear had a bowl for porridge. The great big bear had a great big bowl; the middle-sized bear had a middle-sized bowl; and the little wee bear had a little wee bowl.

Each bear had a chair to sit on. The great big bear had a great big chair; the middle-sized bear had a middle-sized chair; and the little wee bear had a little wee chair.

And each bear had a bed to sleep in. Father Bear had a great big bed; Mother Bear had a middle-sized bed; and Baby Bear had a little wee bed.

One morning Mother Bear made porridge for breakfast and put it into the bowls. It was very hot; so the three bears went for a walk into the wood and left their porridge to cool.

While they were away a little girl came to the cottage. Her name was Goldilocks, for she had bright golden hair. When she saw that no one was at home she lifted the latch and went in.

Goldilocks soon spied the bowls of porridge cooling upon the table. She was hungry after her walk, so the little girl took a taste from the great big bowl of porridge. It was too hot for her. She took a taste from the middle-sized bowl of porridge. It was too cold for her. Then she took a taste from the little wee bowl of porridge. The porridge in it was neither too hot nor too cold, but just right. She liked it so well that she ate it all up.

Then the little girl saw the three chairs beside the wall. She was tired, so she sat down in the great big chair, but it was too hard for her. Then she sat down in the middle-sized chair, but that was too soft for her. Last of all, she sat down in the little wee chair. That was neither too hard nor too soft, but just right. So Goldi-locks seated herself in it. There she sat for such a long time that the seat of the chair came out, and down she went, plump on the ground.

Goldilocks went upstairs into the bedroom in which the bears slept. She was so tired that she lay down upon the great big bed; but it was too high at the head for her. Then she lay down upon the middle-sized bed; but it was too high at the foot for her. Last of all, she lay down upon the little wee bed. That was neither too high at the head nor too high at the foot. It was just right. So she covered herself up and lay there till she fell fast asleep.

Soon the three bears came home. Now Goldilocks had left the great big bear's spoon standing in his porridge. When he saw it he said in his great big voice, "Somebody has been at my porridge!"

When the middle-sized bear saw her spoon standing in her porridge she said in her middle-sized voice,

"Somebody has been at my porridge!"

Then the little wee bear looked at his porridge bowl. The spoon was in it, but the porridge was all gone.

"Somebody has been at my porridge and has eaten it all up!" he said in his little wee voice.

Seeing that some one had entered their house the three bears went round the room. At last they came to the three chairs. Father Bear said in his great big voice,

"Somebody has been sitting in my chair!" For he saw that the cushion had been moved.

Mother Bear saw that her cushion had been moved, too. So she said in her middle-sized voice,

"Somebody has been sitting in my chair!"

You know what Goldilocks had done to Baby Bear's chair. When he saw it he said in his little wee voice,

"Somebody has been sitting in my chair and has broken it!"

Then the three bears went upstairs into their bedrooms. When Goldilocks had tried the great big bed she pulled the pillow out of its place. Father Bear saw this and said in his great big voice,

"Somebody has been lying in my bed!"

Goldilocks had pulled the pillow in the middle-sized bed out of its place, too. And when Mother Bear saw this she said in her middle-sized voice,

"Somebody has been lying in my bed!"

And when Baby Bear came to look at his little wee bed he saw Goldilocks in it fast asleep. So he said, in his little wee voice,

"Somebody has been lying in my bed—and here she is now!"

Baby Bear's voice wakened Goldilocks at once. Up she started. When she saw the three bears she ran to the window. Fortunately, the window was open and it was not far from the ground. Goldilocks jumped out. You may be sure the little girl ran home as fast as she could go.

THE THREE LITTLE PIGS

Once upon a time three little pigs started out to seek their fortune. The first little pig met a man with a bundle of straw, and said to him, "Please, man, give me that straw to build me a house."

The man gave the straw, and the little pig built a house.

By and by the wolf came along and knocked at the door of the little house, and said, "Little pig, little pig, let me come in."

And the little pig said, "No, no, by the hair of my chinny, chin, chin."

And the wolf said, "Then I'll huff, and I'll puff, and I'll blow your house in."

> So he huffed, and he puffed,
> And he blew the house in.
> And he ate up that poor little pig.

The second little pig met a man with a bundle of furze,* and said to him, "Please, man, give me that furze to build me a house."

*Bush branches.

174

The man gave the furze, and the little pig built a house.

By and by the wolf came along and knocked at the door of the little house and said, "Little pig, little pig, let me come in."

The little pig said, "No, no, by the hair of my chinny, chin, chin."

And the wolf said, "Then I'll huff, and I'll puff, and I'll blow your house in."

So he huffed, and he puffed,
And he blew the house in.
And he ate up that poor little pig.

The third little pig met a man with a load of bricks, and he said, "Please, man, give me those bricks to build me a house."

The man gave the bricks, and the little pig built a house.

By and by the wolf came along. He knocked at the door of the little house and said, "Little pig, little pig, let me come in."

The little pig said, "No, no, by the hair of my chinny, chin, chin."

And the wolf said, "Then I'll huff, and I'll puff, and I'll blow your house in."

So he huffed, and he puffed,
And he puffed, and he huffed,
But he could not blow
That pig's house in.

Then he said, "Little pig, I know where there is a field of nice turnips."

"Where?" asked the little pig.

"In the home field. If you will be ready early to-morrow morning I will call for you. We will go together and get some for dinner."

"Very well," said the little pig. "What time shall I be ready?"

"At six o'clock," said the wolf.

The little pig got up at five o'clock, pulled the turnips, and went back home.

The wolf came at six o'clock and called out, "Little pig, are you ready?"

"Ready! I've been and come back. I got a potful of nice turnips for dinner."

The wolf was angry, and he said to himself, "I'll catch that little pig somehow."

So he called out, "Little pig, I know where there is a nice apple tree."

"Where?" asked the little pig.

"In the orchard not far from here," said the wolf. "If you will wait for me I'll come for you at five o'clock to-morrow morning. We will go together and get some for dinner."

But that little pig got up the next morning at four o'clock and hurried off to get the apples. He hoped to get back before the wolf came, but he had far to go and had to climb the tree. Just as he was scrambling down the tree he saw the wolf coming. The little pig was very much frightened. When the wolf came up he said, "Little pig, you are here before me. Are the apples sweet?"

"Very sweet," said the little pig. "I will throw you down one."

He threw an apple far away from the tree. While the wolf was gone to pick it up, the little pig jumped down and ran home.

The next day the wolf came again to the little pig's house and said, "Little pig, there is a fair in the village this afternoon. Will you go?"

"Oh, yes!" said the little pig. "What time shall I be ready?"

"At three," said the wolf.

So the little pig went to the fair before the time. He bought a churn and was hurrying home with it when he saw the wolf coming. He did not know what to do. Then he said to himself, "I'll hide in the churn." He crept in, and by so doing he turned the churn round and round. It began to roll along, and soon it started rolling down the hill with the little pig inside. This so frightened the wolf when he saw it that he ran home without going to the fair.

The next day he went to the pig's house and said, "O little pig, when I was going to the fair I saw a great round thing which came rolling past me down the hill."

"Ha! Ha! Ha!" laughed the little pig. "I frightened you, then, did I? I had been to the fair and bought a churn. When I saw you coming, I got into it and rolled down the hill."

Then the wolf was very angry, and he said, "*I will* eat up that little pig. I'll get down the chimney after him."

When the little pig saw what the wolf meant to do he made up a blazing fire and hung over it a potful of water. Just as the wolf was coming down the chimney the little pig took off the pot-lid and—splash! In fell the wolf! And that was the end of the wicked fellow.

THE THREE BILLY GOATS GRUFF

Once upon a time there were three billy goats. The little one was called Little Billy Goat Gruff. The next older was called Big Billy Goat Gruff and the oldest was called Great Big Billy Goat Gruff.

The goat's home was in a meadow through which ran a brook. On the other side of the brook was a green hillside where the grass was sweet and juicy.

One day Little Billy Goat Gruff said, "I am hungry. There is no grass in this meadow. I shall go over the bridge to the hillside. The sweet juicy grass there will make me fat."

Great Big Billy Goat Gruff said, "A hungry troll lives under that bridge, Little Billy. He is watching for a good dinner. If you cross the bridge he will eat you up."

But Little Billy Goat Gruff was not afraid. He said, "The troll shall not eat me. I am going across the bridge to the hillside and get fat."

Trip trap, trip trap sounded Little Billy's feet as he went over the bridge.

Of course the troll heard him.

"Who trips over my bridge?" called out the angry fellow.

Little Billy Goat Gruff answered in a little voice, "It is I, Little Billy Goat Gruff, tripping over the bridge. I am going to the hillside to make myself fat."

"I am coming to gobble you up," roared the troll.

"Oh, do not eat me now," said Little Billy Goat Gruff. "Wait until I grow fat. Then I shall make you a good dinner."

"Go along, then," said the troll, "I will wait until you grow fat."

Then trip trap, trip trap trotted Little Billy Goat Gruff across the bridge to the hillside where he began to eat the sweet, juicy grass.

When Big Billy Goat Gruff saw Little Billy Goat Gruff eating grass on the hillside he said, "The troll did not eat Little Billy. I shall go over the bridge to the hillside. The sweet juicy grass there will make me fat."

Trip trap, trip trap, trip trap sounded Big Billy Goat Gruff's feet on the bridge. Of course the troll heard him.

"Who trips over my bridge?" called out the big fellow.

Big Billy Goat Gruff answered in a big voice. "It is I, Big Billy Goat Gruff, tripping over the bridge. I am going to the hillside to make myself fat."

"I am coming to gobble you up," roared the troll.

"Oh, do not eat me now," said Big Billy Goat Gruff. "Wait until I grow fat. Then I shall make you a good dinner."

"Go along, then," said the troll, "I will wait until you grow fat."

Then trip trap, trip trap, trip trap trotted Big Billy Goat Gruff across the bridge to the hillside where he began to eat the sweet, juicy grass.

When Great Big Billy Goat Gruff saw Big Billy Goat Gruff eating grass on the hillside he said, "The troll did not eat Big Billy. I shall go over the bridge. The sweet juicy grass on the hillside will make me fat."

Trip trap, trip trap, trip trap, trip trap sounded Great Big Billy Goat Gruff's feet on the bridge. Of course the troll heard him.

"Who trips over my bridge?" he roared.

And in a deep voice Great Big Billy Goat Gruff said,

"It is I, Great Big Billy Goat Gruff, tripping over the bridge. I am going to the hillside to make myself fat."

"I am going to gobble you up," roared the troll.

But Great Big Billy Goat Gruff was not afraid. He said, "Come and eat me, if you can. I want to see you and I want you to see me. I have two big horns upon my head and I can soon strike you dead!"

"I am coming to gobble you up,"roared the troll again.

"Come along then," shouted Great Big Billy Goat Gruff.

The next minute the troll put his head over the side of the bridge. Great Big Billy Goat Gruff put his head down and ran at the troll.   BANG! went Great Big Billy Goat Gruff's head against the troll. Then SPLASH! went the troll tumbling into the water. He sank down and down and down and was never seen again.

Trip trap, trip trap, trip trap, trip trap went Great Big Billy Goat Gruff across the bridge and to the hillside. So the three Billy Goats Gruff ate the grass there and they grew fat.

WHAT FRIGHTENED PETER RABBIT

One bright morning when Peter Rabbit was eating sweet clover in the field something jumped up in front of him. It was big and black and it had two long ears. Wasn't Peter Rabbit frightened! He hopped away as fast as he could go.

He was hurrying along when he met Bushy Squirrel.

"Why are you hopping away so fast, Peter?" asked Bushy.

"O Bushy," said Peter, "when I was eating sweet clover in the field this morning something frightened me."

"Did you see it?" asked Bushy.

"I did," said Peter.

"What did it look like, Peter?"

"It was big and black and it had two long ears. When I hopped it hopped. Can you tell me what it was?"

Bushy Squirrel thought for a moment. Then he said, "Indeed I cannot, Peter. Let us find Brown Hare. He will know what it was that frightened you, I'm sure."

Away went Peter Rabbit and Bushy Squirrel as fast

as they could go. When they reached the woods Brown Hare saw them coming.

"Where are you going so fast, Bushy and Peter?" Brown Hare called out.

"O Brown Hare," said Peter, "I am so frightened. I am running away."

"What is the matter?" asked Brown Hare.

"This morning when I was eating sweet clover in the field something frightened me," said Peter.

"Did you see it?" asked Brown Hare.

"I did," said Peter.

"He did," said Bushy.

"What did it look like, Peter?"

"It was big and black," answered Peter.

"It was," said Bushy Squirrel.

"And it had two long ears," Peter added.

"It had," said Bushy Squirrel.

"Can you tell me what it was, Brown Hare?" asked Peter.

Brown Hare thought for a while; then he said slowly, "I cannot, tell you, Peter Rabbit. Let us go and ask Wise Owl about it."

"We will," said Peter and Bushy.

Away went Peter Rabbit, Bushy Squirrel, and Brown Hare. They soon came to Wise Owl's home in the tree.

"Whoo-oo-who," called out Wise Owl.

"Peter Rabbit, Bushy Squirrel, and Brown Hare," answered the three.

"Why do you come to my tree when it is my bedtime?" asked Wise Owl in a very stern voice.

"O Wise Owl," said Peter Rabbit, "this morning when I was eating sweet clover in the field something frightened me."

"It did," said Bushy.

"Yes, it did," said Brown Hare.

"Did you see it, Peter?" asked Wise Owl then.

"Yes, I saw it," said Peter.

"He did," added Bushy.

"He certainly did," said Brown Hare.

"Tell me what it looked like, Peter," said Wise Owl.

"It was big and black."

"It was," said Bushy.

"It certainly was," added Brown Hare.

"And it had two long ears," Peter went on.

"It had," said Bushy.

"It certainly had," added Brown Hare.

"We have come to ask you what it was," said Peter Rabbit. "Can you tell us?"

Wise Owl put on his glasses and thought for a moment. Then he asked slowly, "You said you were in the field this morning?"

"I was," said Peter.

"He was," said Bushy Squirrel and Brown Hare.

"Was the sun shining, Peter?" asked Wise Owl.

"It was," answered Peter.

"It was," said Bushy Squirrel and Brown Hare.

Then Wise Owl thought again. Soon he burst out laughing and called to Peter, "Run out there in the sunshine, Peter, and turn round and round and round."

Peter Rabbit did as Wise Owl told him to do. As he turned round something jumped in front of him. It was big and black, and it had two long ears. When Peter hopped, it hopped.

"Ha, ha, ha!" laughed Peter. "I was afraid of my own shadow!"

"Your own shadow," said Bushy Squirrel in surprise.

"Afraid of your own shadow," called out Brown Hare in surprise.

Then they all laughed and laughed and laughed.

"Thank you, Wise Owl," said Peter. "I will go back to the field and eat sweet clover."

"Never be afraid of shadows," called out Wise Owl, as Peter Rabbit and Bushy Squirrel and Brown Hare hopped and frisked away.

TABBY AND THE MICE

Three little mice once lived in an old box.

"I am going to make a new house," said the largest mouse, whose name was Rus.

"*I* am going to make a new house," said the next mouse, whose name was Fus.

"*I* am going to make a new house," said the third mouse, whose name was Mus.

"My house shall be made of hay," said Rus, who did not like to be cold.

"My house shall be made of paper," said Fus, who was fond of books.

"My house shall be made of bricks," said Mus, who was as wise as he could be.

So the three little mice made their homes.

One day Tabby Cat came along. She saw the three houses that the little mice had made.

She was a very polite old cat, so she knocked at the door of the first house.

"Come, Mr. Rus; please let me in!" said she.

"Oh, no," said Rus; "you may not come in."

Tabby was a wise old cat. She put her soft paw into the hay and caught Rus.

Then she went to the next house. "Come, Mr. Fus; let me in," she said.

"Oh, no!" said Fus, "you may not come in."

But Tabby knew better than that. She put her paw through the paper door and caught poor Fus. Then she went to the next house.

"Come, Mr. Mus; let me in!" said she.

"Oh, yes!" said Mus; "when I am ready."

So Tabby sat down to wait. She laughed when she thought what a nice supper Mus would make.

When she had waited a long time, she grew tired.

"Are you ready now, Mr. Mus?" she asked.

"Not yet," said Mus.

By and by Tabby knocked loudly on the door.

"I am coming in now, Mr. Mus," said she.

"Very well; come in if you like," said Mus; but he did not open the door.

So Tabby tried and tried to open the door.

Then she tried to push down the house. Then she

tried to make Mus come out.   At last she told Mus just what she thought of him.

This did not trouble Mus at all.   He had curled himself up in a snug corner of his house and was fast asleep.

LITTLE BROWN BEAR AND BIG BILLY GOAT

I

Little Brown Bear had a house of his own. It was in the woods. He had one table, one chair, and one bed. He had one bowl and one spoon for milk. But Little Brown Bear was not happy, because Big Billy Goat who lived in the woods wanted Little Brown Bear's house.

Every day Little Brown Bear went for a walk. When he left he

> Shut the door,
> Turned the lock,
> And put the key into his pocket.

He was afraid of Big Billy Goat.

One morning Little Brown Bear went to hunt for berries. He forgot to

> Shut the door,
> Turned the lock,
> And put the key into his pocket.

Big Billy Goat came along.   He saw the door of Little Brown Bear's house open.   He looked around but he could see no one.

He walked up to the door, opened it a very little way, and put his head in.   Then he opened it a little farther and put one hoof in.   Then he put another hoof in, and another and another.   He was inside Little Brown Bear's house!

He looked around.   "Ha! ha!   This is just what I want," he said.

Big Billy Goat was hungry. He saw a bowl of milk on the table.

"This too is just what I want," he said.

Then he drank all the milk in the bowl.

Big Billy Goat was tired.   He looked around and saw a bed.

"And *this* is just what I want," he said.

He climbed into the bed and tried to lie down.   The bed was too short for him.   He tried to lie across the bed.   It was too narrow for him.

"I cannot lie in this bed one way or the other," said Big Billy Goat.   "So I'll lie under it."

He lay down upon the floor under the bed and was soon fast asleep.

By and by Little Brown Bear came home.   He looked at his bowl.

"Some one has been drinking my milk," he said.

He went to his bed and looked at it.

"Some one has been lying on my bed," he said.

Then he heard a noise under the bed.

"Some one has been lying under my bed," said Little Brown Bear, "and here he is now."

He looked down and saw four feet.   Then he saw two shining eyes.   He knew Big Billy Goat was under the bed.

Little Brown Bear was afraid, but he called out, "Ouff! Ouff!   Get out of my house."

"I shall not get out of your house," said Big Billy Goat.

Little Brown Bear was very much afraid, but again he said, "Ouff! Ouff! Get out of my house."

"This house is mine, now," said Big Billy Goat.

Rap, rap, rap, rap!   He made a great noise with his hoofs on the floor.   At this Little Brown Bear ran out of his house and into the woods.

The first one he met was Red Fox.

"O, Red Fox, please help me. This morning I went to the woods to get berries. When I got home I found Big Billy Goat in my house. He will not go out."

"I am afraid of Big Billy Goat," said Red Fox. "He has great big horns. Ask Gray Wolf to help you."

Little Brown Bear ran on and on. Soon he met Gray Wolf.

"O, Gray Wolf, please help me. This morning I went to the woods to get berries. When I got back, I found Big Billy Goat in my house. He will not go out."

"I am afraid of Big Billy Goat," said Gray Wolf. "He has two big horns. Ask Black Bear to help you."

Little Brown Bear went on saying, "Will no one help me?"

Soon Busy Bee came buzzing by. He heard what Little Brown Bear said.

"Buzz, buzz," said Busy Bee. "I can help you, Little Brown Bear. I will do so. Promise not to take my honey from the tree."

"I promise," said Little Bear. "But how can you make Big Billy Goat go out of my house? Red Fox is afraid of him and Gray Wolf is afraid of him."

"A little bee can sting," he answered.

Away flew Busy Bee to Little Brown Bear's house. Then he went in.

"Buzz, buzz, buzz," he said.

"O, a little bee can sting," thought Big Billy Goat. "This is *not* what I want."

Busy Bee flew around the room, then into Big Billy Goat's ear.

"Get out of my ear. Go away," cried Big Billy Goat.

"Take me out of this house. Then I will get out of your ear," buzzed the bee.

Big Billy Goat scrambled from under the bed. Then he ran out of the house and into the woods as fast as he could go.

Busy Bee flew out of his ear.

"Thank you, Busy Bee," called out Little Brown Bear. Then he hastened into his house. You may be sure that this time he

> Shut the door,
> Turned the lock,
> And put the key into his pocket.

And Big Billy Goat never went into Little Brown Bear's house again.

THE OLD WOMAN AND HER PIG

An old woman was sweeping her house and she found a little crooked sixpence.

"What shall I do with this sixpence?" said she. "I will go to market, and buy a little pig."

So the old woman went to market and bought a pig. And as she was coming home she came to a stile*; but the pig would not go over the stile. So she said:

> "Pig, pig, get over the stile;
> Or I shan't get home to-night."

But the pig would not.

She went a little farther, and she met a dog. So she said to the dog:

> "Dog, dog, bite pig;
> Pig won't get over the stile;
> And I shan't get home to-night."

But the dog would not.

She went a little farther, and she met a stick. So she said:

*Steps for passing over a fence.

> "Stick, stick, beat dog;
>   Dog won't bite pig;
>   Pig won't get over the stile;
>   And I shan't get home to-night."

But the stick would not.

She went a little farther, and she met a fire. So she said:

> "Fire, fire, burn stick;
>   Stick won't beat dog;
>   Dog won't bite pig;
>   Pig won't get over the stile;
>   And I shan't get home to-night."

But the fire would not.

She went a little farther, and she met some water. So she said:

> "Water, water, quench fire;
>   Fire won't burn stick;
>   Stick won't beat dog;
>   Dog won't bite pig;
>   Pig won't get over the stile;
>   And I shan't get home to-night."

But the water would not.

She went a little farther, and she met an ox. So she said:

"Ox, ox, drink water;
Water won't quench fire;
Fire won't burn stick;
Stick won't beat dog,
Dog won't bite pig;
Pig won't get over the stile;
And I shan't get home to-night."

But the ox would not.

She went a little farther, and she met a butcher. So she said:

"Butcher, butcher, kill ox;
Ox won't drink water;
Water won't quench fire;
Fire won't burn stick;
Stick won't beat dog;
Dog won't bite pig;
Pig won't get over the stile;
And I shan't get home to-night."

But the butcher would not.

She went a little farther, and she met a rope. So she said:

"Rope, rope, hang butcher;
 Butcher won't kill ox;
 Ox won't drink water;
 Water won't quench fire;
 Fire won't burn stick;
 Stick won't beat dog;
 Dog won't bite pig;
 Pig won't get over the stile;
 And I shan't get home to-night."

But the rope would not.

She went a little farther, and she met a rat. So she said:

"Rat, rat, gnaw rope;
 Rope won't hang butcher;
 Butcher won't kill ox;
 Ox won't drink water;
 Water won't quench fire;
 Fire won't burn stick;
 Stick won't beat dog;
 Dog won't bite pig;

Pig won't get over the stile;

And I shan't get home to-night."

But the rat would not.

She went a little farther, and she met a cat. So she said:

"Cat, cat, kill rat;

Rat won't gnaw rope;

Rope won't hang butcher;

Butcher won't kill ox;

Ox won't drink water;

Water won't quench fire;

Fire won't burn stick;

Stick won't beat dog;

Dog won't bite pig;

Pig won't get over the stile;

And I shan't get home to-night."

But the cat said to her, "If you will go to yonder cow, and fetch me a saucer of milk, I will kill the rat."

So away went the old woman to the cow, and said:

"Cow, cow, give me a saucer of milk;

Cat won't kill rat;

Rat won't gnaw rope;

Rope won't hang butcher;

Butcher won't kill ox;

Ox won't drink water;

Water won't quench fire;

Fire won't burn stick;

Stick won't beat dog;

Dog won't bite pig;

Pig won't get over the stile;

And I shan't get home to-night."

But the cow said to her, "If you will go to yonder hay-makers, and fetch me a wisp of hay, I'll give you the milk." So away went the old woman to the haymakers, and said:

"Haymakers, give me a wisp of hay;

Cow won't give me milk;

Cat won't kill rat;

Rat won't gnaw rope;

Rope won't hang butcher;

Butcher won't kill ox;

Ox won't drink water;

Water won't quench fire;

Fire won't burn stick;

Stick won't beat dog;

Dog won't bite pig;

Pig won't get over the stile;

And I shan't get home to-night."

But the haymakers said to her, "If you will go to yonder stream, and fetch us a bucket of water, we'll give you the hay."

So away the old woman went; but when she got to the stream, she found that the bucket was full of holes. So she covered the bottom with pebbles, and then filled the bucket with water, and away she went back with it to the haymakers; and they gave her a wisp of hay. As soon as the cow had eaten the hay she gave the old woman the milk; and away she went with it in a saucer to the cat. As soon as the cat had lapped up the milk,

The cat began to kill the rat;

The rat began to gnaw the rope;

The rope began to hang the butcher;

The butcher began to kill the ox;

The ox began to drink the water;

The water began to quench the fire;

The fire began to burn the stick;

The stick began to beat the dog;
The dog began to bite the pig;
The little pig in a fright jumped over the stile;
And so the old woman got home that night.

THE COCK, THE MOUSE, AND THE LITTLE RED HEN

Once upon a time there was a hill, and on the hill there was a pretty little house. It had one little green door and four little windows with green shutters, and in it there lived a Cock and a Mouse and a little Red Hen.

On another hill close by there was another little house. It was very ugly. It had a door that wouldn't shut and two broken windows, and all the paint was off the shutters. And in this house there lived a bold bad Fox and four bad little Foxes.

One morning these four little Foxes came to the big Fox and said:

"Oh, father, we're so hungry."

"We had nothing to eat yesterday," said one.

"And scarcely anything the day before," said another.

"And only half a chicken the day before that," said a third.

"And only two little ducks the day before that," said a fourth.

From "World Stories Retold." Used by permission of George W. Jacobs & Company.

The big Fox shook his head for a long time, for he was thinking. At last he said in a big gruff voice: "On the hill over there I see a house. And in that house there lives a Cock."

"And a Mouse," screamed two of the little Foxes.

"And a little Red Hen," screamed the other two.

"And they are nice and fat," went on the big Fox. "This very day I'll take my great sack and I will go up that hill and into my sack I will put the Cock and the Mouse and the little Ren Hen."

"I'll make a fire to roast the Cock," said one little Fox.

"I'll put on the sauce-pan to boil the hen," said the second.

"And I'll get the frying pan to fry the Mouse," said the third.

"And I'll have the biggest helping when they are all cooked," said the fourth, who was the greediest of all.

So the four little Foxes jumped for joy and the big Fox went to get his sack ready to start upon his journey.

But what was happening to the Cock and the Mouse and the little Red Hen all this time?

Well, sad to say, the Cock and the Mouse had both jumped out of bed on the wrong side that morning. The

Cock said the day was too hot, and the Mouse grumbled because it was too cold.

They came grumbling down to the kitchen where the good little Red Hen, looking as bright as a sunbeam, was bustling about.

"Who'll get some sticks to light the fire with?" she asked.

"I shan't," said the Cock.

"I shan't," said the Mouse.

"Then I'll do it myself," said the little Red Hen.

So off she ran to get the sticks.

"And now, who'll fill the kettle from the spring?" she asked.

"I shan't," said the Cock.

"I shan't," said the Mouse.

"Then I'll do it myself," said the little Red Hen.

And off she ran to fill the kettle.

"And who'll get the breakfast ready?" she asked as she put the kettle on to boil.

"I shan't," said the Cock.

"I shan't," said the Mouse.

"Then I'll do it myself," said the little Red Hen.

During breakfast the Cock and the Mouse quarreled

and grumbled. The Cock upset the milk jug and the Mouse scattered crumbs on the floor.

"Who'll clear away the breakfast?" asked the poor little Red Hen, hoping they would soon leave off being cross.

"I shan't," said the Cock.

"I shan't," said the Mouse.

"Then I'll do it myself," said the little Red Hen.

So she cleared everything away, swept up the crumbs, and brushed up the fireplace.

"And now, who'll help me to make the beds?"

"I shan't," said the Cock.

"I shan't," said the Mouse.

"Then I'll do it myself," said the little Red Hen.

And away she tripped upstairs.

But the lazy Cock and Mouse sat down in a comfortable arm-chair by the fire and soon fell fast asleep.

Now the big Fox had crept up the hill and into the garden, and if the Cock and Mouse hadn't been asleep, they would have seen his sharp eyes peeping in at the window.

"Rat-tat-tat, rat-tat-tat," the Fox knocked at the door.

"Who can that be?" said the Mouse, half opening his eyes.

"Go and look for yourself, if you want to know," said the rude Cock.

"It's the postman, perhaps," thought the Mouse to himself, "and he may have a letter for me." So without waiting to see who it was, he lifted the latch and opened the door.

As soon as he opened it, in jumped the big Fox with a cruel smile upon his face.

"Oh, oh, oh!" squeaked the Mouse, as he tried to run up the chimney.

"Doodle-doodle-do!" screamed the Cock as he jumped upon the back of the biggest arm-chair.

But the Fox only laughed, and without more ado he took the little Mouse by the tail and popped him into the sack, and seized the Cock by the neck and popped him in, too.

Then the poor little Red Hen came running downstairs to see what all the noise was about, and the Fox caught her and put her into the sack with the others. Then he took a long piece of string out of his pocket, wound it round and round and round the mouth of the sack, and tied it very tight, indeed.

After that he threw the sack over his back, and off he set down the hill.

"Oh, I wish I hadn't been so cross," said the Cock as they went bumping about.

"Oh, I wish I hadn't been so lazy," said the Mouse, wiping his eyes with the tip of his tail.

"It's never too late to mend," said the little Red Hen. "And don't be too sad. See, here I have my little work-bag and in it there are a pair of scissors, and a thimble, and a needle and thread. Soon you will see what I am going to do."

Now the sun was very hot. Mr. Fox began to feel his sack was heavy, and at last he thought he would lie down under a tree and go to sleep for a little while. So he threw the sack down with a bump, and very soon fell fast asleep.

Snore, snore, snore! went the Fox.

As soon as the little Red Hen heard this, she took out her scissors and began to snip a hole in the sack just large enough for the Mouse to creep through.

"Quick," she whispered to the Mouse, "run as fast as you can and bring back a stone just as large as yourself."

Out scampered the Mouse and soon came back drag-ging the stone after him.

"Push it in here," said the little Red Hen, and he pushed it in in a twinkling.

Then the little Red Hen snipped away at the hole till it was large enough for the Cock to get through.

"Quick," she said, "run and get a stone as big as yourself."

Out flew the Cock and soon came back quite out of breath with a big stone, which he pushed into the sack, too.

Then the little Red Hen popped out, got a stone as big as herself, and pushed it in. Next she put on her thimble, took out her needle and thread, and sewed up the hole as quickly as ever she could.

When it was done, the Cock and the Mouse and the little Red Hen ran home very fast, shut the shutters, drew down the blinds, and felt quite safe.

The Fox lay fast asleep under the tree for some time, but at last he woke up.

"Dear, dear," he said, rubbing his eyes and then looking at the long shadows on the grass. "How late it is getting. I must hurry home."

So the Fox went grumbling and groaning down the hill till he came to the stream. Splash! in went one foot.

Splash! in went the other foot, but the stones in the sack were so heavy that at the very next step down tumbled Mr. Fox into a deep pool. And then the fishes carried him off to their fairy caves and kept him a prisoner there, so he was never seen again. And the four greedy little foxes had to go to bed without any supper.

But the Cock and the Mouse never grumbled again. They lit the fire, filled the kettle, laid the breakfast, and did all the work, while the good little Red Hen had a holiday and sat resting in the arm-chair.

No foxes ever troubled them again, and, for all I know, they are still living happily in the little house with the green door and green shutters which stands on the hill.

GRANDMOTHER'S VALENTINE

"Secrets, Fido! You must not tell." Jean shook a finger in her little dog's face. "You must not tell any one," she added.

Fido didn't know what secrets were, but he did know that when Jean held up her finger it meant that there was something to be careful about; so he wagged his bit of tail and smothered a bark.

"I'll tell you about it," said Jean, working away busily. "I've made one for Mother, one for Father, one for Jack, one for Susan, and I've six more almost finished. No one but you will see them until St. Valentine's Day, Fido."

Jean counted them again, one by one. "I haven't made one for Grandmother yet," she said thoughtfully. "Her valentine must be the best of them all, Fido, the loveliest and *best*." She looked again at her valentines. They were of all sorts and sizes and colors,—blue, pink, red, and gold. On some she had painted cupids with gauzy wings; others were covered with hearts pierced with tiny darts. One was wreathed with flowers as bright as those that grew in Grandmother's garden.

"They're beautiful," said Jean again, "but not one of them is what I wish for Grandmother. Hers must be different from the others."

Jean had been working all day, painting, cutting, and pasting. It had been easy to make a valentine for the members of her own family and for each one of her little friends; but it was hard to think of one which would carry her message of love to Grandmother. She placed all that she had made in a long row and looked thoughtfully at each one; but she was not satisfied. For some time she sat thinking. Fido wagged his tail and wondered what was the matter.

Suddenly, she jumped to her feet and cried out, "I know what I'll do. But—— O Fido, this time I shall not tell even *you* my secret!"

Fido wagged his tail and watched his little mistress gather up all the hearts, cupids, and paper lace she had left, and put them together. Then she ran upstairs as fast as she could, calling to her little dog who was close at her heels, "Not this time, Fido. You must not come with me this time."

In a moment Jean came down the stairs with something white in her arms. She ran into the next room where she had been making valentines and she locked the door.

As soon as supper was over Jean slipped out of the house and ran to the homes of her little friends in the neighborhood.

Under each door she slipped a valentine. But, strange to say, she did not leave one under Grandmother's door, although Grandmother lived but two houses away.

Next morning when Jean's father went to the door he called out, "Come, come! See what St. Valentine has left for us." There, on the step, lay two beautiful valentines. Jean's mother came running to see the surprise. "There is no name on them," she said. "See the beautiful red hearts and dear little cupids."

Then Fido could keep still no longer. He wagged his stumpy tail as hard as he could and at the same time he leaped and barked with joy.

"Ha! ha!" laughed Mother. "Fido knows St. Valentine has been here. I must run over to Grandmother's and see if she, too, has had a visit from him."

Jean did not say a word, but as soon as her mother had left, the little girl ran to her room, changed her dress, and threw a big cloak about her. Then she and Fido ran as fast as they could to Grandmother's house laughing all the way.

She knocked at the door, threw off her cloak, and waited. She heard Grandmother's voice saying: "That sounds like my little girl's knock. I'm having several visitors this morning."

Grandmother opened the door. There stood Jean in a white dress all covered with red hearts and little cupids with flaming darts. Fido was dancing and barking round her.

In a minute Grandmother knew what it all meant. She threw her arms around her little girl and said:

"This is my valentine,
This is my dove;
This is the child
I dearly love."

KING MIDAS

Long ago there lived a rich king. His name was
Midas. He had one little daughter named Marygold.

King Midas loved gold more than anything else in the
world. He had bags and bags of it which he kept in a
dark room underneath his castle. Every day he would
spend much time alone counting his gold pieces. But no
matter how much gold he had he always wished for more.

One day as he looked at his treasures and bowls and
trunks full of gold, he said, "That is not enough. I wish
I had all the gold in the world."

As he spoke something like a shadow fell across the
floor. He turned quickly to see what it was. There before him stood a man whom King Midas had never seen
before.

"Who are you?" he asked the stranger.

"I am Mercury," was the answer. "I heard your wish,
King Midas. You are a very rich king, are you not?"

"Yes, I have some gold," answered Midas, "but not
enough, not enough!"

A dark frown came upon his face. He looked very unhappy.

"If one wish could be granted to you, King Midas, for what would you ask?"

"I desire to be the richest king in all the world. It would take a long time to gain enough gold to make me happy. So my wish is that everything I touch might turn to gold."

"Ha! ha!" laughed Mercury. "You wish for the Golden Touch. Very well, King Midas, to-morrow morning at sunrise you shall have the Golden Touch!"

That night the king could scarcely sleep for joy. In the morning he jumped out of bed and began to dress. In a flash every garment he touched turned to gold.

"Was ever a king so happy as I?" cried Midas. He ran about the castle touching everything that he passed. When he went for his morning walk he touched the flowers. Immediately they became golden. Even the path and the grass upon which he trod turned to gold.

As he was very hungry he went into the castle for his breakfast. There were fine fish and hot rolls and baked potatoes spread before him. But when he tried to eat them they turned to gold in his mouth. How hungry

King Midas was then! There was plenty of gold for breakfast but he could not eat that!

As the hungry king was sitting before the table, Marygold ran to him. She held a golden rose in her hand. The child was crying bitterly.

"O Father," she said, "some one has spoiled the garden. See this rose!"

Looking up the child caught sight of her father's face. She saw that he was in trouble.

"Dear Father," she cried. "You look so sad. What is the matter?"

She threw her arms about his neck to kiss him. Then a dreadful thing happened. Little Marygold was turned to gold! Even the great tears on her cheeks were golden and her beautiful brown curls were gold and hard.

Oh, how unhappy was King Midas then!

"Marygold, dear, Marygold," he cried.

But Marygold could not answer. She was a golden statue. Poor Midas wrung his hands. He wished he were the poorest man in the world if losing his gold would bring back his little girl.

At that moment Midas heard a merry laugh. There stood Mercury before him.

"What! Are you not happy, King Midas?" asked the fairy.

"Happy? Look! I have changed my little daughter to a golden statue. I shall never be happy again. I beg of you, take away this wretched touch."

"King Midas," said Mercury, "would you rather have the Golden Touch or a cup of cold water?"

"A cup of cold water! Alas! It will never quench my thirst again."

"The Golden Touch or a crust of bread?" continued Mercury.

"A crust of bread is better than a castle full of gold," answered Midas.

"The Golden Touch or your little Marygold?" asked the stranger.

"My little Marygold," cried Midas. "I would rather have her than all the gold in the world! I beg of you, take away this hateful touch."

"You are wiser than you were, King Midas," said Mercury. "I will help you."

He told the king to go to a stream that flowed through the castle gardens and bathe himself in it.

"The water will wash away the Golden Touch," continued Mercury. "Bring to the castle a jug of the same water. Sprinkle it over everything you wish to change back from gold."

Midas lost no time in obeying Mercury. The king plunged into the stream. Then, filling a jug with the precious water, he hastened back to the castle. You may be sure that the golden statue of Marygold was the first thing he sprinkled. How happy King Midas was once more when he saw her open her eyes, laugh, then run into the garden to play.

CLYTIE

Long ago there lived a beautiful nymph named Clytie. Her home was in a cave at the bottom of the sea.

She was a very happy little creature. All day long she played in her lovely garden. She gathered shells and took care of the strange flowers that grew there. Sometimes she chased the little fish that swam about.

Often she went riding through the green waters. When she wished to go swiftly she would hitch two gold fishes to her shell carriage. Then away they would dart through the green waves. Sometimes Clytie enjoyed riding slowly. Then she would hitch two slow moving turtles to her carriage and let them go at their will.

One summer night when the turtles were drawing her along Clytie fell asleep. On waking she found that the turtles had taken her near the shore. The next moment a large wave washed her upon the beach.

Clytie had never seen land before. She stepped out of the shell carriage and sat down upon a rock facing the eastern sky.

It was early morning. Suddenly, Clytie noticed a bright light in the sky. She looked up and saw the brilliant sun in his chariot of gold. He was beginning his day's journey across the heavens.

Clytie could not turn her eyes away from him. Never in her life had she seen anything so beautiful. She forgot about her carriage and her slow moving turtles. She forgot about her home in the sea. All day long her eyes followed the sun until he sank into the west in a cloud of gold.

Day after day she came to the shore to watch the glorious sun. Nothing else made her happy. She wished that she might always live where she could enjoy the beautiful sight.

One day a strange thing happened. Clytie's feet became rooted in the earth. Her body turned into a tall slender stem, and her dress changed into large green leaves. And last of all her face became a beautiful yellow flower. The little sea maiden had changed into a tall sunflower. And to this day she watches the sun in his journey across the sky.

THE GO-TO-SLEEP STORY

"How can I go to bed," said Penny, the flossy dog, "till I say good night to Baby Ray? He gives me part of his bread and milk, and pats me with his little soft hand. It is bedtime now for dogs and babies. I wonder if he is asleep?"

So he trotted along in his silky white nightgown till he found Baby Ray on the porch in mamma's arms.

And she was telling him the same little story that I am telling you:—

"The Doggie that was given him to keep, keep, keep,
Went to see if Baby Ray was asleep, sleep, sleep."

"How can we go to bed," said Snowdrop and Thistledown, the youngest children of Tabby, the cat, "till we have once more looked at Baby Ray? He lets us play with his blocks and ball, and laughs when we climb on the table. It is bedtime now for kitties and dogs and babies. Perhaps we shall find him asleep." And this what the kitties heard:—

"One doggie that was given him to keep, keep, keep,
Two cunning little kitty-cats, creep, creep, creep,
Went to see if Baby Ray was asleep, sleep, sleep."

"How can we go to bed," said the three little bunnies,
"till we have seen Baby Ray?" Then away they went in
their white velvet nightgowns as softly as three flakes of
snow. And they, too, when they got as far as the porch,
heard Baby Ray's mamma telling the same little story:—

"One doggie that was given him to keep, keep, keep,
Two cunning little kitty-cats, creep, creep, creep,
Three pretty little bunnies with a leap, leap, leap,
Went to see if Baby Ray was asleep, sleep, sleep."

"How can we go to bed," said the four white geese,
"till we know that Baby Ray is all right? He loves to
watch us sail on the duck pond, and he brings us corn in
his little blue apron. It is bedtime now for geese and
rabbits and kitties and dogs and babies, and he really
ought to be asleep."

So they waddled away in their white feather night-
gowns, around by the porch, where they saw Baby Ray,
and heard mamma tell the "Go-to-Sleep" Story:—

"One doggie that was given him to keep, keep, keep,
Two cunning little kitty-cats, creep, creep, creep,
Three pretty little bunnies, with a leap, leap, leap,
Four geese from the duck-pond, deep, deep, deep,
Went to see if Baby Ray was asleep, sleep, sleep."

"How can we go to bed," said the five white chicks, "till we have seen Baby Ray one more? He scatters crumbs for us and calls us. Now it is bedtime for chicks and geese and rabbits and kitties and dogs and babies, so little Baby Ray must be asleep."

Then they ran and fluttered in their downy white night-gowns till they came to the porch, where Baby Ray was just closing his eyes, while mamma told the "Go-to-Sleep" Story:—

"One doggie that was given him to keep, keep, keep,
Two cunning little kitty-cats, creep, creep, creep,
Three pretty little bunnies, with a leap, leap, leap,
Four geese from the duck-pond, deep, deep, deep,
Five downy little chicks, crying, 'peep, peep, peep,'
All saw that Baby Ray was asleep, sleep, sleep."

THE LITTLE CHILD'S GOOD NIGHT

The sun is hidden from our sight,
  The birds are sleeping sound;
'Tis time to say to all, "Good night!"
  And give a kiss all round.

Good night! my father, mother, dear:
  Now kiss your little one;
Good night! my friends, both far and near;
  Good night to every one!

Good night! ye merry, merry birds:
  Sleep well till morning light;
Perhaps if you could sing in words,
  You would have said, "Good night!"

To all my pretty flowers, good night!
  You blossom while I sleep;
And all the stars that shine so bright
  With you their watches keep.

The moon is lighting up the skies,
The stars are sparkling there;
'Tis time to shut our weary eyes,
And say our evening prayer.